Murder in Limehouse

Book 5

A Dodo Dorchester Mystery

By

Ann Sutton

Published by

Wild Poppy Publishing LLC
Highland, UT 84003

Distributed by Wild Poppy Publishing

Cover design by Julie Matern
Cover Design ©2021 Wild Poppy Publishing LLC

Edited by Jolene Perry

Dedicated to
Raymond Sutton

Author's Note

Do you ever have moments where you know God is telling you that you are on the right path? Let me tell you about my recent ones with the writing of this book.

Coming up with names for minor characters is not like trying to name a baby but it has to *feel* right. Sometimes the names come in a flash of inspiration and other times I am scrolling through lists and last names trying to find one that jumps out at me.

Such was the case with the murder victim in Murder in Limehouse. The name Stella came in a flash but I was struggling with a last name. While scrolling, I found the name Stanhope. It was good, solid and not too common.

Next, I wanted Rupert to live in a little mews house in London. Mews houses were built for grooms during the Victorian era when grand families moved to the capital for a season. With little land, they needed somewhere to house their horses.

As motor vehicles replaced horses, the houses became fashionable residences and are so still today.

I googled 'Mews in London' and the very first one that popped up was 'Stanhope Mews'!! I was stunned. What were the chances?

Obviously, I couldn't use that one as it was now my murder victim's name so I scrolled on, my heart beating just a little faster after my first discovery. I stopped at Cresswell Place Mews and began to read the blurb about it and dropped my virtual pencil. Guess who lived at number 22?

AGATHA CHRISTIE!

So, of course, Rupert had to live there!

I thought that's where this amazing story ended until a month or so later.

I sent the manuscript to my beta readers. The first one called to discuss with me her thoughts about the book, and while we were chatting, I received a text from her. I clicked on it and it was a picture of a very handsome young man.

"Who is this?" I asked her.

"He is a friend of mine, He is Finnish and you will never guess his name. Rupert!"

I almost dropped the phone. Rupert is not a Finnish name and there aren't many people called that at all these days. I cannot share the photo with you because I have not received permission but let me just tell you that he is the perfect model for Rupert, down to the blond curl that flops across his forehead and the chipped tooth!

Wow, just wow!

Style Note

I am a naturalized American citizen born and raised in the United Kingdom. I have readers in America, the UK, Australia, Canada and beyond. But my book is set in the United Kingdom.

So which version of English should I choose?

I chose American English as it is my biggest audience, my family learns this English and my editor suggested it was the most logical.

This leads to criticism from those in other English-speaking countries, but I have neither the time nor the resources to do a special edition for each country.

I do use British words, phrases and idioms whenever I can (unless my editor does not understand them and then it behooves me to change it so that it is not confusing to my readers).

Table of Contents

hree days.

Three days had passed since they had parted and not a peep.

No message waiting for her at home. No nothing.

Had she misread the situation? Was he merely playing with her affections?

The hundred-year-old grandfather clock struck the hour in the vast entry of Beresford House, sending its deep timbre through the walls, the echo ricocheting round the cavernous hall just as her emotions were ricocheting around her mind.

A heavy sigh escaped as she glared at the ornate clock on the mantle in the sitting room.

Why hasn't he called?

With one scarlet nail Dodo absentmindedly pushed the scattered design sketches from the House of Dubois around the smooth mahogany table without seeing any of them.

"Have you heard one word I've said?" asked Didi, who had been chattering away about her latest holiday.

Dodo tore her eyes from the timepiece and puckered her plump, red lips. "I'm so sorry, darling little sister. You are quite right; I have ignored you frightfully. No excuses." Her lips curved into a smile of apology. "Would you mind repeating yourself?"

"I think I would rather hear what, or rather who, has *you* so distracted. Come on, out with it!" Didi's cornflower blue eyes were bursting with anticipation in her doll-like face.

As a rule, the two sisters were very close, but life had taken some unexpected turns of late, and Dodo had not had the occasion nor the energy to confide in her beloved Didi. Just fourteen months apart, they had been inseparable as children, right up until Dodo went to finishing school in Paris after the end of the war, but adult life kept pulling them apart.

1

Didi Dorchester was the perfect complement to her sister; where her sister was dark, she was blonde, where Dodo was tall, Didi was petite. But there was a fresh innocence about Didi that centered Dodo. Her heart squeezed as she realized how much she had missed her sister through all the trauma of the last few weeks.

Contemplating her sister's delightful face, she wondered if at this point, there was actually much to tell.

"Is it that obvious?" Dodo asked, chuckling.

"To cite a cliché: as the nose on your face," replied Didi, laughing.

Not one to beat around the bush, Dodo began her confession. "His name is Rupert. Rupert Danforth III."

"Should I know him?" Didi asked, her golden curls bouncing with curiosity.

"I didn't," Dodo replied. "I'm actually amazed that our paths have never crossed before."

The aristocracy was not as small a population as most commoners imagined and there were many tiers. But still.

Didi made a bridge with her slender hands upon which to rest her perfect chin, eyes wide with interest. "Go on."

Dodo explained about rushing down to Blackwood Manor on the Devonshire moors, home of their twin cousins, and meeting Rupert, whom she dismissed as a fool from the moment she met him.

"Why?" interrupted Didi. "Does he have one of those insanely high-pitched, nasally voices?" Her brows shot up with amusement as she waited for clarification.

"No..." Dodo made a dramatic pause. "He arrived with Veronica." She had no need to explain to her sister about whom she was talking. Her history with the vindictive, vicious girl was well known to Didi.

"No!" Her features were etched with horror.

"Yes!"

"Then why are you wasting any time on him?" The light curls were trembling with indignation. "He is clearly more than a tad deficient in the head."

Dodo let out a sharp burst of laughter at her sister's well-placed scorn. She reached out a hand and placed it affectionately over Didi's. "You always have been my most fervent defender."

Dodo explained about the murder that had taken place during her stay at Blackwood and how her investigation had uncovered the truth that the relationship between Rupert and Veronica was only a ruse; that Veronica had simply coerced Rupert into *pretending* to be her beau.

Didi placed both palms on the table. "Well, now I just feel sorry for the poor chap." Her eyes flew to Dodo's. "But whyever would Veronica do that? And why would this chap, Rupert, agree? She is so incredibly horrid!"

The thought of explaining about her break-up with Charlie, who was a friend of them both, and her dalliance with Chief Inspector Blood, which she felt more than a little guilty about, was just too much right now. She would divulge all of that when she felt up to it. An edited version of the truth was all she could manage at present.

"Veronica bumped into Bunty at a polo match, and she boasted that I was her cousin, if you can believe it."

"I can!" declared Didi. "I brag about being your sister all the time."

"Do you really?" Her sister's unexpected comment dragged her fully out of her reverie.

"Of course! Lady detective, fashion guru. I'm incredibly proud of you, Dodo."

Dodo's hand went to her chest. "I had no idea. I'm flattered."

"Anyway…?" prodded Didi.

"Bunty mentioned that I was popping down, and Veronica saw it as a chance to prove something."

Didi slapped the table, her hand landing on the pressed and folded newspaper that awaited their father's perusal. "Just like Veronica! Childish!" Normally a levelheaded girl, such was the effect Veronica had on the kindest of people.

A coil of gratification unfurled in Dodo's stomach as she watched her sister rise to her defense. *How do people get through life without a sister?*

Dodo waved a hand. "It's all forgotten now," she said. "If Veronica hadn't come, I would not have met Rupert and…" Didi's features sharpened with expectation. "I have never met a man quite like him." Dodo traced the headline on the Times. "He *does* things to me." She placed a palm to her chest. "Here."

Didi's expression registered shock and interest. "I should very much like to meet this man who has such power over you." Didi pushed the newspaper to the side. "And you are waiting for him to call?"

"You have hit the proverbial nail on the head." She spread out her palms. "It's been *three* days."

Didi's eyes crinkled with mirth. "Three days? That's not so very long. He probably doesn't want to appear too eager. You know how men are."

She did. Dodo had gone through a lot of men in the last year. She made a half-hearted attempt at gathering the sketches together. "I do, but he's not like most men. He wouldn't play those silly games." *At least I don't* think *he would.*

Didi tipped her head. "A man who does not play games. Now I'm *really* intrigued."

Dodo began to explain that Rupert had gone to Blackwood with Veronica to help his sister who was addicted to opium and had got herself into a spot of bother, when the delightful sound of the telephone floated through the door.

She stopped mid-sentence, her heart hitching.

Didi allowed the silence, watching her sister with amused eyes.

After a few moments, the firm step of the butler could be heard, creaking on the hardwood floor. As the door handle to the breakfast room moved down, Dodo's gaze fixed on it as though it held all the answers to the universe.

"Lady Dorothea," Sanderson began, his voice as stiff as his posture. "You are wanted on the telephone."

Dodo jumped up, knocking her chair to the floor in her haste. She threw back a smile of satisfaction to her sister and hurried from the room. As she approached the telephone cabinet her heart was thudding pleasantly against her ribs.

"Hello!" she said a little breathlessly.

4

"Hello, darling!"

"Oh! David." Her heart dropped.

She and David Bellamy were old friends and normally a call from him would be highly valued.

The tone on the other end turned to ice. "Am I to infer that I was *not* the person you were expecting?"

Dodo gave a little shake of her head. "Oh, David! You are *always* a welcome voice at the end of the telephone. It's just that I've been waiting for a call from someone…"

David's tone perked up. "A *male* someone?" He loved any and all gossip, which was why he was such a valuable asset in her sleuthing.

Dodo looked at her reflection in the window of the telephone booth and smoothed her hair. "As a matter of fact, yes."

The chill in his voice melted away like frost on a warm spring morning. "Tell Uncle David everything."

Dodo filled him in on her latest conquest. "Do you happen to know him?"

"Not personally," he replied, "but I have heard the family name mentioned on occasion. Is he worthy of you?"

David had made it clear on more than one occasion that he would like to move from his status as a friend to something much more, but Dodo had always shut him down. David was too important as a friend and mixing friendship with romance was a recipe for disaster in her experience. Besides, as handsome as he was, David did not set her heart aflutter.

"Yes, David. He *is* worthy."

"But he hasn't called…" David was not above rubbing things in.

"No."

"How long has it been?" David asked.

"Three days." She fingered a pearl stud earring. "He said he would take me to the theater, but I haven't heard a thing."

David huffed through the line. "Three days is nothing, old thing."

"But he seemed so eager." she persisted. "If you met someone you liked how long would *you* wait?"

She could see David wrinkling his aquiline nose in her mind's eye. "I would have to make myself wait at least two days so as not to appear too keen."

"And it's been three," she pointed out. "Perhaps I misread the situation."

"Perhaps," he agreed. "Tell me more."

Dodo repeated the tale of how they met with more details.

"I love stories where the couple hates each other at first," said David.

Dodo cleared her throat. "I don't think *he* ever hated *me*," she corrected. "He was playing a part and had to appear uninterested."

"Because no one could ever hate *you*, darling," said David, his tone laced with sarcasm.

"That is *not* what I meant, and you know it!" she retorted. "I just meant that he was paying someone back for helping his sister and part of the bargain was that he would play the devoted boyfriend."

"Tell me again what happened before he left," said David.

Dodo bit her cheek, resting her forehead against the cool glass. "He said he would call me and set up a date for the theater."

"I mean before that. Before that awful Veronica woman interrupted him."

Dodo's ruby lips curved into a devilish smile. "He was leaning in for a kiss."

"He's serious then." Dodo could hear him slapping his desk. "If he was merely making small talk, he wouldn't have tried to kiss you."

"I know. Honestly, you could have cut the romantic tension with a knife." She drummed the glass window with polished nails. "But why hasn't he called?"

"Have you tried to contact him?"

Dodo frowned. "That is just not done, David. I have my reputation to think of. I am not accustomed to begging men to take me out. And I will not begin now. Not even for him."

David laughed so hard she could picture him falling off his chair. "You've got that right. You are perhaps *the* most eligible lady in town."

"I think my reach goes farther than that," she teased.

"Touché!" David became serious. "Now, what do we know about him?"

"Not much, actually. I know his name, Rupert Danforth, and that he has two younger sisters. One is called Julia, I think."

David coughed. "I do have some expertise in the area of research, you may recall."

"Oh, David. I couldn't possibly!"

Dodo ignored the snort from the other end of the line. "Well, if you change your mind, you know where to find me."

She made a kissing noise.

"Now, the reason I called…" David began.

"Of course, *you* called *me!*" cried Dodo. "What can I do for you?"

"Speaking of debts to pay…do you remember promising to accompany me to my cousin Daphne's wedding?"

Chapter 2

As Dodo hurried along Regent's Street toward Livery's of London, a bulky portfolio clasped in one hand and a cumbersome umbrella in the other, the rain turned to sleet.

Fabulous! My least favorite weather.

She gritted her teeth.

Dashing past newspaper boys standing beside soggy headline posters that screamed about the problem of morphine in the capital city, the fat, black print jogged her memory of a similar headline on her father's paper the day before.

She was due to meet with the sales purchaser of Livery's who was interested in some of Renée Dubois' designs. Dodo was an ambassador for the House of Dubois in Paris, a position her mother was in two minds about.

The beautiful Tudor revival building that was Livery's stood proud despite the gloomy weather, the sooty black timbers emphasizing the architecture perfectly. She clambered up the wet steps, closing her black umbrella and shaking the rain off. A distinctive doorman in a green uniform trimmed with gold, opened the door.

"Lady Dorothea Dorchester to see Miss Stella Stanhope," she said, awkwardly offering him her card as she tried to keep hold of everything.

"This way m'lady," he replied.

She followed him through the perfume department with its heavenly scents and across the men's shoe floor to a brass, scissor-gated lift manned by another uniformed employee. The first man handed the young lift operator Dodo's card and explained her appointment.

With a smile on his friendly, good-looking face, the lift attendant drew the scissor gate back, motioning for Dodo to enter.

"Billy Blake at your service." He drew the gate back and pressed the button for her floor, tunelessly whistling as they began their ascent. It sounded more like birdsong than music.

"Miss Stanhope is on the fourth floor." He had a brilliant smile that matched her own, and his eyes sparkled with enough mischief to indicate that he would be a popular companion.

"Here we are, m'lady. Fourth floor. Miss Stanhope's office is the third door on the right. Follow me."

She stepped out after him into a narrow, stale corridor lined with large, oak doors each bearing a brass name plate. The floor dipped a little.

This was Dodo's first-time meeting with Stella Stanhope and though Renée Dubois had already broken into Livery's market, her exposure was still small. She was hoping that Dodo could expand their account with the world-renowned store. Dodo adjusted the leather portfolio as the personable lift attendant, Billy, knocked.

"Come in!" The voice was as pleasant as a dentist's drill.

Billy shot Dodo a grimace as he held open the door and Dodo entered a surprisingly expansive but chaotic office with a low, beamed ceiling. The space was bursting with every kind of colorful fabric swatch imaginable.

The woman sitting behind the desk laid down her long, black cigarette holder, glared at Dodo over thick, black rimmed glasses and cracked a false smile.

Dodo hoped the smoke would not make her sneeze.

"Lady Dorothea, *do* sit down."

Dodo felt as welcome as an undertaker at a wedding. A leather club chair sat opposite the desk and Dodo glanced at the soggy umbrella in her hand.

"There's a holder by the door," barked Miss Stanhope.

Dodo looked back and saw a modern, black lacquer tube and quickly placed the wet article in it then perched on the edge of the deep, masculine chair.

"You have some sketches, I understand." Elbow on the desk she opened her hand to receive the leather case.

The woman was as warm as a northeaster wind.

Dodo tried to read Stella's expression as she studied each sketch. The small, dark eyes roved around each picture as the lips tightened around large front teeth, giving nothing away. After a few seconds perusal Stella would drop the picture and grab

9

another. Dodo examined the room whose messiness was at odds with its occupant. She reigned in the impulse to touch the fabrics that lay within arm's reach. Sleet slid down the leaded windows; a reminder that the atmosphere outside was even less welcoming than in this office.

"This one!" The woman stabbed the picture with a sharp, pink, highly polished nail, startling Dodo.

She snapped her eyes back to the desk. Stella was pointing to a dark trouser suit with boxy shoulders and a bow in place of a tie. It was the most androgenous of the designs and Dodo's least favorite.

"I think this will be very popular. Women are seeking to appear less feminine in my opinion."

Dodo couldn't disagree more, but her job here was to sell Renée's work regardless of her own feelings about the designs.

"Can you have it ready for sale by January?" She peered at Dodo over the black frames.

It was early November and Dodo knew that Renee's business model was to have the designs sewn and ready so that she could pre-empt other houses that needed some lag time. It was risky but had worked for Renée thus far.

"Of course," said Dodo, wondering why the woman in front of her spent so much time on her nails and so little time on her short, flat hair.

Stella placed the suit design to the side and continued her brief examination of the other sketches. She had already discarded Dodo's favorite evening gown of antiqued lace. Her eyes narrowed to the point that Dodo was doubtful she could still actually see the pictures on the pages.

No small talk.

No commentary.

"This!" Her speech was so abrupt and sharp that it grated on Dodo.

Stella had chosen a dress that would be appropriate for the races or a garden party. Renée had daringly raised the hems of the spring dresses even farther. Just three years ago the new fashions still clung to the ankles but as one new year gave way to another, the hem lines crept ever up.

10

As Stella continued to inspect each design, Dodo felt at liberty to examine the brusque woman's dull, dark hair which was cut like a man's but with less precision. The edges were ragged, and the style had no body. It did the wearer no favors. How had such a severe woman reached the heights of fashion purchaser for one of the most prestigious department stores in the world?

"And these." At last Stella had chosen some feminine daywear that Dodo would have been happy to model.

Dodo put the woman's age at forty but her inability to smile had led to severe lines around her austere mouth.

She gathered the pictures, marking the back of the sketches that had been chosen, then reached to shake Stella's hand. After regarding Dodo's hand with a scowl, Stella stretched out her own and Dodo caught a flash of a small tattoo on her wrist.

Her grip was firm and a little painful. When they released, Stella grabbed the cigarette holder and clamped it between her yellowed teeth. Dodo disliked cigarettes herself but Renée used a cigarette holder and managed to make it look like a glamourous and daring accessory. Stella just looked cold and harsh. Dodo could feel the smoke tingling her nose. It was time to leave.

"Goodbye." There seemed little point in attempting polite conversation with the woman who merely nodded back. The whole interview had taken less than fifteen minutes.

When Dodo stepped out of the office, Billy was leaning against the frame of the lift. Seeing her he stood to attention, pulling down his uniform. He pulled back the scissor gate.

"Have you been waiting for me?" she asked.

"Sorta. Miss Stanhope never sees anyone for more than fifteen minutes, so I watch the clock and make sure I'm up here." A saucy grin crept along his mouth. "She would have my guts for garters if I wasn't."

"Sensible boy." She bestowed upon him one of her patented smiles. He melted under its power and touched his cap as she walked into the lift.

"What do you think of Miss Stanhope?" she asked him.

Billy cast nervous eyes at Dodo and quickly looked at the ground. "She gets the job done, I'll say." He pressed the button

11

that would take them down to the ground floor and Dodo decided to leave the poor boy alone.

As she stood back on the wet steps of the department store, she was relieved to see that the sleet had stopped.

Drat! I left my umbrella upstairs.

She went back in, apologizing to the doorman and tucking the large portfolio under her arm. Billy started when he saw her.

"Didn't expect to see you again so soon, m'lady."

"I forgot my blasted umbrella," she explained as he drew the gate back.

They rode up in silence as the boy whistled quietly. "Fourth floor!" he chirped and slowly drew back the gate. She strode over to Stella's door and knocked.

"Enter!"

Dodo walked in and Stella's eyes widened. Her mouth was slack and her expression vacant and Dodo fought the urge to stare.

"Yes?" Stella's voice was still sharp, but it had lost its cutting edge.

"I forgot my umbrella," Dodo said, turning to the lacquer cannister and retrieving the apparatus.

Stella's head appeared too heavy for her neck.

"Goodbye," said Dodo.

"Yes," replied Stella Stanhope, her lids drooping slightly.

Dodo exited and closed the door, pausing with her hand on the handle, bothered by something she could not quite put her finger on.

What had caused the Jekyll and Hyde transformation?

Chapter 3

The journey back to Beresford House was dreary. The cloud cover was thick, and the train was crowded. Dodo decided that she should have taken the car and a driver or stayed in town until the weather improved. Exhausted, the gentle rocking of the train lulled her to sleep until a dream about Stella trying to blow cigarette smoke into her face had woken her with a jolt just before arrival at the Little Puddleton station.

She had not called home to let them know when she was arriving and took a taxi back from the station. After paying the driver she slumped through the large front door into the familiar vestibule where the scent of roast beef from the kitchens made her stomach grumble. She shoved the portfolio onto the hall table and slid off to the drawing room in search of a refreshing tipple. Her mother and Didi were already there enjoying the warmth of the fire.

"Darling! You look absolutely dreadful! Come and sit by mumsy." Her mother, Lady Guinevere Dorchester, patted the silver settee. "How was town?"

"Ghastly," Dodo replied kicking off her shoes and placing her aching feet on a little poof and wiggling her toes. "Didi, would you mind?"

Her sister rolled her eyes but went to make a fortifying cocktail.

Lady Guinevere placed a comforting arm around her oldest daughter. "Tell me all about it."

Dodo relished any opportunity to embellish a tale and had both her sister and mother laughing in no time.

"Miss Stanhope was dressed like a man?" asked her mother smoothing her own, extraordinarily feminine dinner gown.

"It's all the rage at the moment, Mummy," said Didi as she handed her sister the glass and sat across from them.

"Whyever would any woman want to do that?" she asked, her enchanting eyes popping out of her head. "I cannot see the draw of trousers, myself. There is no room for one's legs to breathe."

"Quite so, Mummy," said Dodo as she closed her eyes after a restoring sip. "But times are changing."

"Well, I don't like it." Lady Guinevere fingered the delicate gold chain around her slender neck.

"This Stella woman sounds simply dreadful," added Didi, plumping up a silk cushion before sitting. "Will you have to work with her again?"

"I sincerely hope not!" Dodo stretched out the arm that held the cocktail. "But I cannot figure out what was wrong when I popped back."

Lady Guinevere patted her perfectly coiffed hair. "It's probably opium."

Both daughters snapped their heads to face her. Dodo's mother generally avoided reality at all possible costs, even going to the point of refusing to listen to or read newspaper articles she found distasteful.

"What?" she asked, pushing her curls back from her forehead. "I don't live under a rock you know," she continued. Dodo and Didi exchanged a look. "Your father was reading the newspaper yesterday and the headline was about the problems of opium in Limehouse—Chinatown, they call it—and he happened to make a comment. There are opium dens from the late 1800s that still operate and encourage a very lowly crowd, but there are a few that cater to a higher clientele. Addiction is a big problem and now it is affecting good families, families like ours."

Dodo thought of Rupert, whose sister was an addict. He still hadn't called, and it made her stomach drop.

"Perhaps this Stanhope woman took some laudanum or something after you left, and you witnessed the immediate effects. I am sure her position is very demanding, and she may feel the need of a little extra oomph."

Dodo's mind went back to the headlines on the streets in London and the newspaper she had ignored the morning before. How would the woman possibly continue to do a good job if she was addicted to opium? She shivered.

"Did anyone call for me?" Dodo was going for nonchalant, but the pity in Didi's face indicated that she had failed.

"I don't know," replied her mother. "Ask Sanderson."

14

The door opened with hardly any sound, and the butler entered to announce dinner.

Dodo's spirits sagged. She looked down at her wrinkled, red day frock. "Do I have to dress for dinner?"

"No, darling," said her mother. "It's just us tonight and you were very late home. You're fine as you are."

Dodo dragged her weary body from the sofa and slipped the black, heeled shoes back on her sore feet. As she followed her mother and sister out of the room Sanderson coughed. She fixed him with a cool blue eye.

"Yes?"

"A Mr. Rupert Danforth called this afternoon and left his number, m'lady."

Her heart hiccupped and the cloak of fatigue slipped to the floor.

Sanderson looked down his hooked nose. "He asked that you call back when you returned home."

Her first impulse was to rush to the telephone cabinet in the hall but that would never do. She had already broken one cardinal rule by not dressing for dinner. She would be hard pressed to get away with breaking another by being late for dinner and her mother would not look upon the slight with favor. Rupert would have to wait, but her appetite had vanished, replaced by a small army of butterflies doing the tango in her tummy.

She walked into the family dining room where her father was already seated and kissed his square head. He looked her up and down with disapproval.

"Dodo has only just returned from London and is bone-weary," said her mother, noticing her husband's distress. "I told her we could make an exception just this once. You don't mind, do you, sweetheart?"

Lord Alfred Dorchester looked very much like he did mind, with bushy white brows that pinched into a 'v', but he held his tongue and nodded. He rarely contradicted his wife.

"Tell Daddy about London," encouraged her mother in an effort to move the conversation from the topic of Dodo's rebellion.

Dodo recited her story again, this time with much less wit.

15

"I think the woman must be one of those opium addicts they were reporting about in the paper," said Lady Guinevere, digging into a crisp, golden Yorkshire pudding.

Lord Dorchester's bushy mustache shot up to tickle his nose. "Could very well be," he agreed. "I think there will have to be some sort of regulation of the stuff," he said, tucking into the roast beef, drowning in rich, brown gravy.

Dodo attempted a morsel but found she could eat none of it. Her foot was bouncing up and down of its own accord.

"What is that infernal noise?" asked her father, turning his head to listen for the annoying sound, knife and fork suspended in mid-air.

Dodo placed a hand on her leg.

The conversation turned to more mundane things and Dodo tapped her plate with a fork. Her father stared at it.

"Sorry."

"Is there somewhere you need to be?" he demanded.

Everyone stopped eating.

"No. Not at all." She placed the fork on the tablecloth and took a gulp of red wine. Didi frowned, head to the side. Dodo merely smiled back.

Everyone ate their dinner painstakingly slowly and dawdled over the dessert which was a particularly fine crème brûlée.

At last, her father called for the port.

The three women slid back their chairs to return to the drawing room.

"Sanderson told me that I need to call someone back," she said, purposely keeping her words vague.

"That blasted telephone," said her mother as she pushed into the warm and inviting room. "I shall never understand why people don't write anymore." Her voice faded as the door closed behind her and Didi.

Dodo rushed to the telephone cabinet and stopped sharp. Her nerves were all in a tangle. Such was the man's effect on her. She took a deep breath and closed her eyes.

You are an intelligent, sophisticated, modern woman.

She sat on the padded bench and carefully reached for the ivory hand piece as her pulse thrummed in her ear. The phone number had been written in excellent cursive handwriting and left on the notepad beside the telephone.

"Kensington 242," she said when the operator got on the line.

"Putting you through," said the friendly, efficient voice.

She could hear ringing on the other end and a shot of anticipation flooded her veins. On and on it rang. She stared at the candlestick stem of the telephone willing someone to reply.

It had now been four days since she had last seen him at Blackwood Manor and the wait caused the tangle in her stomach to become a full-blown knot.

"Danforth." He was a little out of breath and Dodo imagined the stray lock of hair that often fell across his forehead.

"Rupert."

"Dodo!" At the sound of his enthusiasm the knot slid undone, and the stresses of the day drained away.

"Sanderson said you had called." No mention of the four long days that had passed.

"Yes! I must apologize for not calling sooner." He dropped his voice. "I had a bit of trouble with my sister again and had to bring her to my place. She is here right now and needs a lot of attention. Can you forgive me?"

Frankly, she had never felt more inclined to forgive anyone. "Of course. I quite understand. I've been rather busy myself." And for the third time she shared the story of her day in town in the rain.

"Jeepers! I have never known anyone who had such an important job before."

She twirled a lock of jet-black hair around her finger. "I'm not sure that fashion can be described as *important*, but I suppose the right clothes do help people to feel more confident."

Rupert huffed. "You're just being modest. Look, I'm desperate to see you again. How about meeting me in town for the theater tomorrow night. I managed to get seats for the new Noel Coward."

"I've been longing to see it!" she cried.

"Meet me at the Savoy Theater at seven and we'll go out to dinner after."

"See you then."

She replaced the ivory handpiece and hugged herself. A chance for a bit of real, uncomplicated fun.

And he was desperate to see her.

Chapter 4

The Savoy Theater was located in Covent Gardens. The spot had been the site of two palaces, a hospital and a military prison, eventually housing a theater for opera in 1880. And it was the first public building to be lit by electric lights. The exterior was red brick and Portland stone; the interior Italian Renaissance with white, pale yellow and gold everywhere but without the usual statues and cherubs. In 1889 an hotel had been attached to the theater.

The original gold satin curtain still graced the stage, and the boxes were red with dark blue seats. Horse-shoe shaped seating gave a perfect view of the stage from every angle.

And Dodo loved it.

As the old theater came into view, she spotted Rupert through the crowd of theatergoers and shoppers, his frame towering above the rest of humanity, the tilt of his head already dear and familiar. A thrill of excitement grabbed her as she stopped to watch him looking for her. Finally, she was attracted to someone from her own class, not someone forbidden, a man who generated the electric charge she knew it was possible to experience. He appeared to be her equal in every way and she knew that when they were seen together, heads would turn, and people would stare.

He swung in her direction, still not seeing her, and she had a moment to study him. His was a face molded by the gods with divine fingers and golden paintbrushes. Even Michelangelo's David could not compete with such perfection, perfection that was beautifully offset by the unexpected chip in his front tooth.

Though she was reluctant to break the enchantment, she ached for the spark of his touch and finally lifted her hand to attract his attention. As he caught sight of her, his face lit up and claimed her with those eyes, sending heat racing through her bloodstream. He looked delicious in a great coat that sat beautifully on his broad shoulders, and an evening suit that was pressed with expert precision.

"Rupert," she said as the crowd heading into the theater faded into obscurity.

"Dodo." His deep rumbling voice infused her name with such tenderness that in spite of her previous experience telling her to slow down, she felt herself falling in love. He leaned in to leave a lingering kiss on her cheek and the softness of his freshly shaven skin and the scent of pine made her yearn for more. "You look better than I remember," he whispered, his voice ragged with emotion. "And I have done a lot of remembering."

All the worry that she had misunderstood his intentions or that the attraction was one sided, melted away. She was used to the men experiencing all the angst at the beginning of relationships, but with Rupert the tables were turned.

"Thank you," she purred.

He brushed his knuckle across her lips, and she shivered.

"I've missed you," he confessed. "Only my sister's situation kept me from calling you earlier— and I didn't want to seem like a lovesick fool by calling too soon."

She tipped back her head and laughed.

"You have done something different," he said, studying her eyes. "I like it."

Always one to dress to impress, she had been particularly careful this evening, choosing a gown that clung to her hips and experimenting with the new smoky eye look that framed her sapphire blue eyes with a contrast that made them shine more than usual.

Offering his arm, they climbed the steps to the entrance, handed their coats to the cloakroom attendant and found their seats. He had reserved a box with an amazing view of the stage and just the right amount of privacy. Feeling a little rebellious, she slipped off her gloves.

As the electric lights went down in the historic theater, and the actors on the stage began to speak, Dodo's stomach flipped as Rupert's hand slid lightly down her bare arm, leaving a trail of goose bumps in its wake. Though she was making a half-hearted attempt to rein in her snowballing feelings, it had never been a gift of hers.

20

Rupert's soft fingers came to rest on her wrist, causing her skin to leap in response and she turned her hand so that their fingers interlaced, never letting her eyes leave the stage.

Dodo was vaguely aware that the actors in the play were speaking, and the audience was laughing, but every one of her senses was engaged in drinking in the man next to her leaving no space in her brain to follow the action below.

It was increasingly obvious that she had met her match. In the short time she had known him, he had proven to be intelligent, kind, considerate and funny. But her attraction to him was something more mystical, something that could not be explained by reason. She had always rejected the notion of a soul mate, but Rupert had unleashed something in her that craved his company and she suspected that he had already succeeded in engraving his soul on hers.

He suddenly laughed at the comedy on the stage and the sound was so magical that she wanted to make him laugh just to bask in it again.

She risked a peek, fearful that her betraying eyes would give away the depth of her feelings and reveal the secret that she already adored him. But she need not have feared for he was looking at her and the intensity of her own emotions was reflected in his eyes. He squeezed her hand, tracing a finger along her cheek.

The play was the Noel Coward, *The Young Idea*, a comedy she had been dying to see but it was as unimportant to her at this moment as a swimsuit at the North Pole.

When the audience applauded, and the lights went up for intermission, she was taken completely by surprise. He turned to her, and his eyes said a thousand things without a single word passing from his lips.

"It's rather amusing don't you think?" he said after a moment, with a smile so sweet she felt the urge to kiss it from his face.

"Jolly fun!" she replied, hoping that he didn't ask her favorite part.

"Ready for a drink?" His left brow rose in an expression so endearing it melted her heart. How could she have ever dismissed him?

He guided her out of the box and down the staircase with long, easy strides, pulling her through the throng and over to the bar.

"What would you like?" he asked, releasing her hand to attract the attention of the barkeep. That was how little they really knew each other— he didn't even know her favorite drink.

"I'll take a *Hanky Panky*," she said, bobbing her black hair with the empty hand.

Failing to catch the barman's eye, Rupert lifted a hand high above the other customers. At six feet four inches he had an advantage few could boast. "I'll take a *Hanky Panky* and a *Southside*," he said, finally succeeding.

While Rupert jostled with the people at the bar, Dodo turned around. The small bar area was chock full of thirsty theatergoers but as she ran a quick eye over them, she didn't see anyone that she knew.

A woman bumped her elbow wearing a hideous feathered turban and it reminded her of Veronica Shufflebottom and how she had first met Rupert. She chuckled.

"Here you go." His velvet voice snapped her back as he lifted the drink over the other patron's head's and brought it to her level. "Let's find a seat over there." He pointed to a private little alcove, and she shimmied through the crowd.

She slid into the white brocade chair and placed her glass on a coaster that bore the Savoy emblem. He dropped smoothly into the chair opposite. The black suit he wore was expertly tailored, with a tight, white bow tie and she was a sucker for a man in a dinner suit. His sandy, thick hair was brushed back revealing a strong, proud forehead.

"You look amazing," he began as he took a little sip of the cocktail.

"You've told me that already," she said, relishing the compliment. She did not tell him that she had tried on three outfits before being satisfied, which made her maid, Lizzie giggle. She had eventually settled on a new dress that the British designer, Hartnell, had sent for her to wear in public as a way to advertise. It had appealed to her because it was out of the ordinary, with an uneven hem that rose to the knee on one side and dipped to the floor on the other. The tiny straps held up a blunt neckline that boasted a sparkling crystal encrusted front panel and a sash in a complimentary color, slung around her hips with a tasteful bow. A decadent kaftan wrap completed the dress. "But I will never stop you telling me again." Her lips curled in a seductive smile and she saw his eyes flash. "I rather like it."

"Now, tell me everything about yourself," he said. "I want to know it all."

She raised one plucked brow as she lifted her gold watch. "In five minutes?"

He huffed, feigning deep disappointment. "Alright, everything you can fit in five minutes."

Dodo puckered her lips.

He looked at them with a longing she recognized. They had been interrupted at Blackwood and the unfinished kiss hung between them.

She drew a finger under her pout and watched as his Adam's apple bobbed.

"I have a darling sister, Diantha," she began. "We call her Didi. You will simply love her."

"Does she look like you?" he asked.

"Not in the slightest. Where I am dark, she is blonde. Where my hair is straight, hers is curly. I love her to pieces."

Reaching out to touch her fingers he said, "Then I cannot wait to meet her."

His lips parted to reveal the small chip in his front tooth.

"How did you do that?" she asked, pointing.

He briefly touched the offending appendage with a shadow of insecurity. "I thought we were talking about you?" The same finger traced along her wrist and her stomach clenched.

"But I want to know all about you too," she said, taking a sip of her own cocktail but keeping her eyes firmly on his.

"I clipped it with my mallet when I was learning to play polo. I was fourteen. I should probably see if I can get a dentist to fix it."

"Oh, don't!" she said quickly. "I like it."

Rupert wrinkled his nose. "Really? Then I won't." The lights flashed indicating that it was time to head back inside to the play.

He tipped his head. "What do you think about skipping the rest and going straight to dinner?"

A feline smile crept onto her lips. "You read my mind."

The tiny restaurant in Pimlico was sophisticated yet understated and bathed in romantically low lights. Rupert pulled her through the narrow door and the maître d' raised his arms in a Latin welcome. They were obviously not strangers.

"And 'oo eez this?" he said, smiling from ear to ear.

Rupert placed a protective arm around her. "Marco, allow me to introduce Lady Dorothea Dorchester."

Dodo lifted her hand and Marco caught it as though it were a rare butterfly, leaning over to place the lightest of kisses, his long mustache tickling her skin.

"Any friend of Senor Danforth, eez a friend of mine," he said, retaining her hand, and swaddling it with his other, capturing Dodo in his charming charisma.

"That is very kind of you, Marco." She bestowed on him her signature smile and watched as his knees buckled. Stunned, his gaze passed to Rupert, still cradling her hand.

"Such beauty. Zis one is a keeper, no?"

Rupert turned soft eyes that burned with pride and a vulnerable hope, on her. "I certainly hope so, Marco, old chap."

"May I take your coat," asked the restauranteur.

Dodo unbuttoned her fur and removed the silky kaftan beneath, as the low candle lights reflected off the shimmering crystals on her bodice.

"Your usual table, senor? Zis way."

Usual?

The intimate establishment contained only seven tables and she wondered who had been here with him before as an arrow of jealousy shot through her. All the tables were designed for just two occupants, with old French chairs made of plaster covered in gold leaf, and damask fabric. Most of the tables were filled with quiet, young lovers and Puccini played on a gramophone player.

As they slid into a table tucked into the back, Marco vanished, and Rupert took her hand.

"Your usual table?" she asked with a pout.

"Marco is just teasing," he grinned. "I mostly come here with one of my sisters, though I have been known to bring the odd girl or two."

"Veronica?"

He shivered. "Crikey, no!" He narrowed his eyes as her pout melted into a wry smile. "Ah, you are teasing me."

"Yes. Now tell me, what is the best thing on the menu? I'm famished."

They ordered and ate, and the romantic tension that had heightened in the theater loosened like a lace on a shoe, allowing for more relaxed conversation. Though Dodo was no stranger to going out with young men, she could not remember a time when conversation had flowed quite so naturally.

She told him how she had become an ambassador for the fashion House of Dubois, and he sat fascinated as she recounted the murder cases she had worked on during the year. He told her of his love of horses and fast cars, and she relished his enthusiasm for polo as they shared a decadent tiramisu.

"So, you have no problem with a woman working?" she asked.

"Great heavens, no!" he declared. "Put that intelligence to good use, I say."

Nice to look at and *a forward thinker*.

She offered him her spoonful.

Dodo's mother kept a fashionable apartment in Mayfair, her 'hidey hole' she called it, and everyone in the family had a key. The moniker was woefully inaccurate as the dwelling had soaring ceilings, massive chandeliers, huge windows, and four bedrooms. It could have housed half of Chelsea if necessary.

Hoping that the evening at the theater would be followed by walks in the park and lunches by the Thames, Dodo had come up with Lizzie that morning.

She had invited Rupert up after dinner and they were now snuggled together on the overstuffed couch listening to jazz on the gramophone.

Dodo was hoping to create an atmosphere where they could get to their unfinished business.

As the needle scratched to the end, Dodo reluctantly peeled herself free. "Would you like a drink? I should have asked before, but I don't drink more than one cocktail and one glass of wine per day. It's a rule of mine."

"How very self-disciplined of you," Rupert said.

"I just know my limits, and I always want to be in control," she said as she went to find another record.

"Always?" A smile tugged at his lips.

She cut her eyes over to him. "Always."

Holding out her hand as the next record began, he stood and took her in his arms, swaying to the sultry sounds of the saxophone.

She laid her head on his chest, the regular beat of his heart tapping her cheek. She was more and more convinced that Rupert was just the right mix of Chief Inspector Blood and Charlie Chadworth. *Could he be the one?*

As the music flowed over them, she felt his finger search for her chin and gently tilt her face. Her heart hitched in anticipation. She was more than ready. He closed the gap between them, and a little gasp escaped as she felt the light touch of his lips on her mouth. His kiss was gentle and undemanding and filled her with warmth from her head to her toes. It had been worth the wait.

When he pulled away to check her reaction, his eyes were overflowing with affection, and she gave her answer by slipping her hand to the back of his head and pulling him to her. He responded by kissing her thoroughly and utterly until she thought she might collapse in a state of happy delirium.

After several delicious minutes he broke the kiss, laughter lines fanning from those gorgeous eyes.

"What?" she asked.

26

"Not *always* in control then." He chuckled.

"I suppose not," she said with a smile that would not be stopped.

She laid her head back in the place nature had carved out for her on his chest and he drew a finger lightly across her brow.

"I can't wait to introduce you to my sisters," he whispered into her hair. "I may have already mentioned you to Julia and she was all screams. She follows you in the society magazines – knew exactly who you were."

"I'm flattered," she murmured.

The record stopped and the needle made the scratching sound but neither of them moved. He kissed her again and she felt as though she were floating.

The clock struck one.

"I'd better go," he groaned.

"I suppose so," she agreed. "When will I see you again?"

"I have some business to attend to tomorrow." He frowned. "How about the National Gallery the day after?"

"Fabulous," she replied, then placing the back of her hand to her forehead like the best dramatic actresses, she said, "and I will try to bear the wait as best I can."

He returned the teasing with a wickedly devastating smile, and she felt herself fall further under his spell.

At the door he kissed the tip of her nose. "Till I see you again."

She could hardly wait.

Chapter 5

With Rupert occupied for the day, Dodo was at liberty to fulfill her obligation to David Bellamy for his help with one of her cases.

No expense had been spared for the wedding of the Earl of Shropshire's only daughter, Daphne. The ceremony had been quite small having taken place in the tiny private chapel inside the wall of the Tower of London. But the reception was quite another matter. Dodo had stopped counting at five hundred. Champagne flowed like water and gastronomical delicacies were abundant. The fragrance of flowers was heady.

The bride, David's cousin, was short and round and looked like an eager head girl from high school. She wore a satin gown that had been expertly tailored to hide any lumps and bumps and an enormous cathedral train. She had not stopped smiling at her tall, thin husband and her rosy cheeks were surrounded by an abundance of curly, dark hair that was framed with a beautiful lace veil that lay atop the train.

Dodo approved.

Jazz music was currently blaring from the band on the stage, and David took her hand with a question in his eyes.

"Of course," she said with a smile.

David was good at many things and dancing was one of them. He could take a left footed, myopic octogenarian and make them appear to be a Josephine Baker. His confident hand led her to the floor and as the music slowed, he drew her to him and smiled down at her. His perfect teeth and blond, manicured hair had her wondering for the hundredth time why his charming face did not ignite anything in her. He was a catch by any definition.

"I know I badgered you into accompanying me to this wedding, but I hope you are having a good time," he whispered in her ear.

"You did not badger me. I came quite willingly. Your help with my cases is beyond comparison, David. And besides, I will probably need your help in the future. No one has their ear to the ground like you do."

"You mean I'm the biggest gossip in town." His right brow quirked.

"If the shoe fits…"

"Did that chap, Rodney or is it Raeburn—?"

"His name is Rupert, as you well know."

"Roooopert," he emphasized, "ever call?"

"As a matter of fact, he did. We went to the Noel Coward at the Savoy and then to dinner."

"Noel Coward! I've been trying to get tickets but it's impossible. He must be connected," David declared with respect in his tone.

"We didn't stay," said Dodo dropping her gaze and feeling a little uncomfortable.

David peered at her. "Didn't stay?"

"Oh, David, we are so good together. We have so much in common and he is exceptionally handsome and…"

David put up a hand. "I have heard quite enough about the competition, thank you. I'm surprised he could spare you."

The beads on the hem of her gown, grazed her ankles as she swayed. "He had some business to attend to today."

David's green eyes narrowed.

"He does!" she cried. "Don't be so suspicious."

David swung her round. "So it was all fireworks and palpitations?" His expression was that of a big brother teasing a younger sister.

"As a matter of fact, yes."

David's hand dropped a little as it held hers. "Really?"

"Really. As you know I have a checkered past with men, but Rupert is…different."

"Well, I wish him the best. Of course, if you would just give *me* a chance, I believe I could take you to the moon." He dipped her suddenly, making her laugh.

When she was back upright, her lips curled. "You know I love you, David, just not in that way."

"Too bad," he huffed, with a wink

A voice boomed over the loudspeakers. "The bride and groom will now cut the cake."

"Do you need to go over there?" Dodo asked, releasing her hand from David's hold and tucking her jet-black bob behind her pearl studded ear.

David chuckled. "No. I've hardly spent three weeks total with this cousin. She won't notice if I'm not there."

They walked back to their table while the rest of the guests crowded around the cake cutting. David picked up his champagne flute and twirled the golden liquid. "I may have done some digging."

Dodo snapped her eyes back to David's debonair face. "You did *what*?"

"Even though my love is unrequited, I worry about you, darling," he said, hand to chest. "I wanted to make sure he was as worthy as you believe. One can't be too careful these days."

A cheer and applause indicated that the knife had made its way successfully through the five-tiered cake.

Dodo shook her head. "I asked you not to."

"You did. But I could not resist." He dropped his eyes and puckered his lips like a guilty dog.

Dodo looked past his shoulder. "So?"

David's face relaxed into a grin of relief. "Attended Harrow and was an above average student." He stopped and checked Dodo's tolerance.

"Go on."

"The war stopped his entry to university—he had earned a place at Cambridge reading the classics—and he was sent to France arriving just after his eighteenth birthday in August 1918. Of course, the war ended in November, so he was lucky not to see too much action. He was chiefly engaged in clean up."

David shuddered. He had not fared so well. Having turned eighteen in 1916, he had seen two years of action and carried a piece of shrapnel in his thigh as a souvenir. Dodo touched his hand.

"Not nearly as screwed up as me," he said with a wobbly grin. He ran his finger around the top of the glass and paused. "I did hear that his sister has a bit of a problem," he said, his voice tentative.

Dodo leaned back in her chair. "I know, he told me himself," she said. "In fact, her 'problem' is why he came to Blackwood in the first place. She had done some shoplifting while…" she hesitated thinking of the best way to sanitize the facts. "…less than accountable for her actions. Veronica's father helped sweep it under the rug. Rupert owed her."

"Ahh," said David. "Yes, his family is quite respectable. Live in some fortress in Leicestershire. Much older than my family. Perhaps not yours."

The voice announced that the bride would be throwing her bouquet.

"That's your cue." David wiggled his eyebrows, and she could not help but laugh.

Though she felt a little sheepish she asked, "Is that all?"

"For now," he replied.

"Right." Getting to her feet and adjusting her jeweled bandeau, Dodo dutifully joined the other bright young things on the floor behind the bride.

As the colorful flowers sailed through the air, she reached out her arms. She was taller than the other girls and her heels gave her even more of an advantage. But the bouquet bounced off her fingers and into the arms of a girl who could not have been more than sixteen. She turned a pained face to David who thought it was jolly funny.

I hope that's not an omen.

Chapter 6

Lizzie breezed in with breakfast on a tray, energy leaping off her.

Dodo had arrived back late from the wedding and a quick glance at the clock told her that it was far too early to be up after a night out. She groaned and rolled over, pulling the soft covers over her head.

"You'll never guess what has happened," Lizzie began, placing the tray on the bed and opening the thick curtains. A gray morning greeted them.

"And a good morning to you too!" quipped Dodo, squinting against the unwelcome day.

"I know it's early, m'lady, but you are going to want to see this. Look! Look at the paper!" cried Lizzie, pointing.

Lizzie was not prone to hysterics—at least not when she was performing her maid's tasks, and Dodo's curiosity was piqued. She pushed herself upright and glanced down to see that there was, indeed, a paper on her breakfast tray. This was out of the ordinary. She grabbed it as Lizzie prattled on. "The criers were shouting it out loud when I went to get breakfast and when I heard what it was all about—well, you'll see soon enough."

She was making no sense at all.

Dodo blinked to clear her eyes of sleep and unfolded the paper. The headline screamed in bold, black type,

'Buyer at Livery of London Dead in Limehouse!'

Dodo snapped her head up to Lizzie. "I told you," Lizzie said, her large eyes wide as dinner plates.

Something shifted in Dodo's stomach, and she pushed the food away, hungry for more details of the murder.

Stella Stanhope, aged 38, was found dead in Limehouse late last night. Her stomach clenched. *Stella!*

She continued reading.

Her presence in the less salubrious area of London's East End is, in itself, a mystery and police are questioning inhabitants and merchants in the area.

The rest of the article went on to detail the woman's rise within the structure of the famous department store. Stella had begun as a salesgirl and worked her way up to the top.

"I was just with her," Dodo cried.

"Exactly! That's why I bought the paper," said Lizzie.

"Stella is…dead." Even speaking the words out loud did not help her process the information. "She was going to buy some of Renée's designs."

"And what on earth was a lady like her doing in Limehouse of all places?" asked Lizzie. "It's a sleazy, dangerous place."

"Yes." Dodo was tapping the page with her finger. "They call it Chinatown. It's where the sailor's land and…satisfy their cravings."

"Wicked," pronounced Lizzie who had been a faithful Sunday School attendee as a child.

"My mother was just talking about the problems in Limehouse," Dodo murmured.

Lizzie stopped what she was doing. "Lady Guinevere was talking about a nasty place like Limehouse?" asked Lizzie "Now that's a surprise," she continued. "Her ladyship usually avoids such things like the plague."

"I know," agreed Dodo. "But something about it caught her attention. She said that it was an area for drugs and was touching even good families like our own." She thought of Rupert's sister.

"Perhaps one of her friends has been affected." Lizzie was setting out all the hair styling tools as she spoke.

"That would explain it," said Dodo, sliding her legs off the bed.

Lizzie pulled some clothes out of the wardrobe and laid them over a chair. "I wonder who caught the case? Do you think it will be…" She let the sentence hang.

"Blood." Dodo supplied the name of the chief inspector who had done curious things to her heart. Just saying his name caused a spike in her pulse, but she was happy to realize that he had less power over her since she had met Rupert Danforth.

"Perhaps he will work it. His expertise is murder, isn't it?" Lizzie raised a brow in warning.

"Possibly." Dodo refolded the paper and put it back on the tray.

Even though she was more used to murder than the average person, knowing that someone she had just met had died in suspicious circumstances was unsettling. And puzzling. She pushed down a hankering to get involved. Other than having met the woman recently, she had no other connection to the case and should stay well away.

Besides, walking back into Blood's life was a bad idea. A very bad idea.

Chapter 7

Standing on the steps of the National Gallery, Dodo looked up at Nelson's Column. It had rained earlier and the scent of it hung in the air. The gray sky was studded with puffy clouds and a stiff breeze blew them across the celestial landscape. Pigeons circled the black lions that guarded the column and fountains as if they owned the place, which of course they did.

She scanned the crowd searching for the familiar blond hair and her heart skipped as she caught sight of his tall frame leaping up the steps two at a time. She had tried not to be early but had failed. The need for punctuality was a blessing and a curse.

"Dodo!" Her name on his lips infused her with such a sense of belonging.

She waved. "Rupert!"

He reached for her hands and placed a chaste kiss on her cheek, then looked approvingly at her fitted jacket, plush, fur collar, and pillar box red cloche hat.

"Dash it all!" he declared and pulling her close, planted a proper kiss right on her lips in front of the whole world.

He pulled back. "I can't tell you how good it is to see you again!"

She threaded her arm through his. "Did you get everything taken care of yesterday?"

"Yes! All set. Now, what did you do while we were apart? I have to confess to having developed an acute interest in every detail of your life for some reason." Lines of happiness carved joy across his features and she felt all her senses come alive.

"I went to a wedding with a friend," she replied taking his arm.

His mouth turned down. "And how was that?"

"Fun actually."

They walked arm-in-arm into a wide gallery and faced the Rembrandt painting *Belshazzar's Feast*. The way the artist captured the sense of surprise on the king's face never ceased to amaze Dodo.

"Do you remember me telling you that I did some work for Renée—the owner of the House of Dubois—with a buyer at Livery's?" she asked as they sailed past a Gainsborough of two children chasing a butterfly. She had seen it many times and did not need to read the plaque.

"Uh huh."

"Did I tell you that the woman was rather prickly, and only had me in her office for fifteen minutes and then unceremoniously ushered me out the door?"

"I remember you mentioning that she was not very friendly."

"Well…" She slowly turned to face Rupert. "She's dead."

Rupert stopped and snapped his eyes to Dodo's face. "Dead?"

"Yes. It's all over today's newspapers, and the criers are yelling about it from pillar to post. You must have seen them."

Rupert frowned. "I was in a hurry; eager to see you, but now that you mention it, I did notice a hullaballoo, though I didn't really pay it any attention. What was her name?"

"Stella Stanhope. She was unmarried and only thirty-eight according to the article I read. It's awful."

He studied her face, seeming to take her concern personally. "How did she die?"

"I don't know. The article didn't say but it was in Limehouse of all places."

Rupert bit his cheek. "What would a career woman who works for one of the most prestigious stores in the world be doing in Limehouse? It's full of opium dens and houses of ill repute."

"I know!" Dodo stopped in front of the *Triumph of Pan*. Her eyes grew wide.

"Could she have had a secret life?" Rupert asked her, oblivious of the great work of art in front of him.

"That is one theory—she could have been an…addict." She was reluctant to mention a subject that was so personal to him.

His expression turned grave. "Yes, that is much more likely."

"The day of the interview, I had to go back to her office to get my umbrella," said Dodo, "and Stella seemed odd, not herself. Her eyes were glassy. Now I am wondering if she had taken something after I left."

A crowd had gathered around the painting, and they moved on. "High powered jobs require nerves of steel I would imagine," said Rupert. "Perhaps she took something for courage."

"She wouldn't be the first," agreed Dodo.

They wandered further into the spacious galleries, past Vemeers and a Gentileschi. Rupert barely looked at the pictures keeping his gaze firmly on her. She enjoyed his attention and since her mother had brought her to the National Gallery regularly as a child, the paintings were as familiar as old friends, and she didn't feel the need to examine them today.

The rest of the museum was practically empty and they swept from room to room, Dodo commenting on this and that artist, until they reached the end in record time for her.

"I'm starving," said Rupert checking his watch. "How about some lunch?"

They ran down the stone steps outside the museum and crossed the street to Leicester Square. Rupert ducked into the first restaurant he saw. A light rain had begun to fall, and the warmth of the little place sent plumes of steam rising from their coats amid the scent of fragrant garlic.

Rupert glanced around as he shrugged off his wool coat. "Sorry, Italian again. Is that alright?"

The voice in her head surprised her by saying, "*I don't care where we eat as long as I'm with you.*" But she merely said, "Perfect!"

"Table for two?" asked a waiter dressed all in black with a white tea towel tucked into his waistband. He was a far cry from Mario. "Follow me."

He seated them at a small table near the front and handed them each a large menu. After taking their drink order he disappeared into the back.

"My mother thinks I must be half Italian," Rupert chuckled. "I could honestly eat Italian food every day."

"I love it too," she agreed. "But I am rather partial to French cuisine."

"I like their sauces but I'm not a fan of their cheese. Give me a good old English cheddar any day."

Dodo dipped her chin. "I shall make it my mission to convert you," she said with a wink.

Scanning the menu, she settled on cannelloni. Rupert took his time deciding and was not ready when the waiter returned.

"I'll just have what she's having," he blurted out.

"Whereabouts in Kensington do you live?" she asked when they were alone again. There was still so much she did not know.

"I have a house in a little mews. A great uncle left it to me as he died '*without issue*' as they say. It's the perfect bachelor pad."

"Do you see your family often?" Family was so important to her, she had to know.

"They live in Leicestershire, and I try and go for Sunday dinner at least once a month. My sisters beg me to go more often but during polo season it's pretty impossible."

"Ah yes, polo," she said. "I am looking forward to seeing you in action."

He dragged a fork across the white tablecloth. "I wouldn't want you to think I am in any way a spectacular player," he said, looking up. "I'm pretty average." The word sparked a memory from her conversation with David. Rupert laced his fingers through hers. "What about you? Where do your people live? Any plans to move out of the family home?"

A vision of Granny popped into Dodo's head. As forward thinking as the Dowager was by the standards of her day, she did not approve of young women living alone, especially not in London. It was not good for the reputation. And Dodo did not have any plans to the contrary. She loved her mother and father and being with her sister. She really had no intention of leaving.

"No. When I want to get away there is always Mummy's flat. My parents are not the oppressive type."

Rupert scrunched his straight nose revealing the endearing chipped tooth again. She felt the strangest urge to reach out and touch it.

"My father is a live-and-let-live type of person, but Mother can be a little smothering. I moved out when I got back from the war," he said.

Dodo squeezed his hand. "Tell me about it—if you can."

Many young men of her acquaintance would do anything rather than talk about their experiences in the Great War, David Bellamy included. But she hoped Rupert's service had left him more intact.

His brows rose in arcs. "I was fortunate. I missed all the fighting, really," he began. "It was almost over by the time I got there, and I was jolly relieved, if you must know. I have a cousin who was invalided out because he lost a foot to the trenches and another who had his eye shot out. I was terrified when it was my turn. And I did see some awful things; men who were shells of their former selves. But my love of horses saved me, as it happens. The army had decided to destroy most of them rather than ship them back, which was an atrocity of unprecedented proportions in my mind, and I wasn't having that. I yelled in the right faces and became the horses' champion. After all those animals had done for our men, it was sacrilegious to shoot them. I made such a fuss that one of the higher ups tasked me with finding homes among the French farmers for as many as I could. I couldn't save them all, of course, but I did my best, I can tell you." His passion for the subject brought color to his cheeks. "Gutted me to see some of their injuries. I took great care to send them to farmers who would let them live out their retirement in peace." His eyes misted over, and she felt her heart wring in her chest. She worried that she should not have harrowed up the memories. But then his face broke into a soft smile, and it was as if the room had been dark and the sun came out. "My broken French improved in leaps and bounds as I advocated for the poor beasts. It was emotionally draining but rewarding work."

The waiter returned with their food and the talk turned to the mundane.

"I have a confession to make," said Dodo after allowing him some time to recover.

He lifted an eyebrow and she fell one step further in love. "I don't ride."

Rupert threw down his serviette and made to stand up. "That is a deal breaker."

Dodo's heart caught in her throat. Then he plonked back down with a huge grin. The relief she felt was enormous.

"I was only teasing," he said. "But from the look on your face it was misplaced. My apologies." He squeezed her hand. "May I ask why?"

It was unheard of for a young woman from the upper classes not to ride. Dodo explained about her accident when she was young that had bred a fear of riding in her.

"I love horses," she hastened to explain. "I just don't love riding them."

"I would be honored to help you overcome your fear," he said, brushing her thumb with his, and sending a lovely ripple up her arm.

"I would be happy to let you."

Usually, when out with a young man Dodo would emphasize her sophistication, her woman of the world persona, but with Rupert she felt no such need.

"What shall we do now?" she said as the sky outside brightened.

Rupert's bright demeanor faded as he glanced at his watch. "I would love nothing more than to spend the entire day with you, but Beatrice is at my house…she had a relapse and I need to chaperone her, make sure she stays off the stuff. She is struggling with withdrawal."

"I could—"

He reached his long fingers up and touched them to her lips setting them humming. "Trust me when I say that Beatrice is not ready for introductions. If it were Julia, I would have brought her to lunch, but Beatrice? She is at a critical juncture and looks bally awful – though if you tell her I said so, I shall deny it."

"Of course." She was surprised by the avalanche of disappointment. She had organized her affairs so as to be at Rupert's disposal.

"I promised Bea I wouldn't leave her alone tonight, but we could meet for lunch tomorrow wherever you like."

She clasped her hands below her chin. "There is a little pub in Greenwich that I'd love to take you to," she said. "It's too cold for sailing which is my favorite way to get there but I can meet you there at one."

"It's a date."

Rupert paid for lunch, and as they emerged from the restaurant the sun decided to put in an appearance.

"Feel like a stroll to the river? I've got time," he said.

"If you're sure?"

He placed his hands on her shoulders. "I'm actually more sure about you than anything in my life right now—" He hesitated looking vulnerable. "Was that too much?"

"No!" she exclaimed. "I feel exactly the same."

Rupert kissed her gently and she felt...complete. She was happy in her independence, but she was not above admitting that Rupert had filled a hole. The security of knowing that their feelings were mutual settled around her shoulders like a warm cape.

The sun was never really warm at this time of year, but it was trying its best. When they crossed the short distance to the river, Rupert dragged her to a secluded iron bench.

"Dodo, I want you to meet my family so much, but I want it to be at their best. Right now, Bea is not at her best and the rest of the family are in the dark. Can you wait?"

She laid her head on his shoulder. "Of course. It's early days yet. Perhaps you can meet my family first."

"I'd be delighted." They sat in companionable silence watching the river flow by, then she lifted her chin ever so slightly and he pressed his mouth to hers. She didn't want it to end.

"I feel like such a boy when I am with you," he said as he touched his head to hers. "I have never felt like this, Dodo. Never."

"Me too," she murmured, eyes closed.

He slid his arms around her and pulled her tight, kissing her thoroughly until her brain was mush.

Big Ben struck the hour as the sun touched the top of the buildings across the river.

Rupert groaned. "I don't want to go but I must. I'll see you tomorrow."

He stood and let his fingers slide through hers.

"Tomorrow," she whispered.

41

Chapter 8

A friendly fire was crackling in the small, green-tiled fireplace, warming Dodo's toes as she drank her tea. Lizzie, was sitting in the armchair on the other side of the fire, knitting. A quiet jazz number was playing on the gramophone and the drapes were drawn against the dark and chill.

"So, you like him, then?" asked Lizzie, counting her stitches.

"I do!" said Dodo, smiling contentedly.

Lizzie stopped counting, dropped her chin and looked up. "Perhaps you will be saying that at the altar in the not-too-distant future."

"Now, now," said Dodo. "Let's not get ahead of ourselves."

"You do make a fine couple," said Lizzie, her tone wistful. "And I could stand seeing that face every day."

Dodo chuckled. "He *is* exceptionally handsome. We went to the National Gallery and all I really wanted to do was look at him."

Lizzie fixed her eyes back on her needles. "I do remember a time at Blackwood when I was the only one singing his praises."

Dodo swatted the air. "That's all in the past. How was I to know that it was all an act? No, the real Rupert is infinitely better than the fake one. We have plans to meet again for lunch tomorrow." She lifted her shoulders with delight and dunked a Digestive biscuit into the tea.

The clack of the knitting needles resumed. "I was a bit surprised to see you back so early. I thought the two of you would do something this evening, to be honest. That's why I had nothing in to eat."

"He had to help his sister, Beatrice. The one with the little problem with opium." She wiped some crumbs from her pleated, blue wool skirt.

The clacking stopped again. "How many men would do so much for their younger sister? I know my brother Ralph wouldn't do all that for me. It shows a quality of character that is charming."

"You can stop singing his praises," Dodo said. "He has already won me over."

The music stopped and Lizzie laid down the scarf she was knitting.

"I'll get it," said Dodo, placing her cup and saucer on the floor next to the comfy chair. She padded over in her stockinged feet and looked through her mother's records. "How about *Cuban Moon?*"

"Lovely," replied Lizzie.

Dodo loved the informality of the hidey hole. No staff were kept on at the flat, but a lady came to set the fires, get in milk and bread and air the place if anyone was coming. No airs, no graces. The line between the classes was more blurred here and Lizzie could relax.

"I won't leave until around eleven in the morning," Dodo said as she swung the needle round and set it on the vinyl. The comforting scratch filled the room, followed by the deep baritone of a trumpet. "What will you do after I leave?"

"Ooh, don't you worry about me," Lizzie said. "I've got plans to visit the market on Carnaby Street. I've heard it's more colorful than the one at home." An impish grin slid across her face.

"I would say that was an understatement," said Dodo.

"Where are *you* going?" Lizzie asked. "There are so many romantic places in London."

"Greenwich."

Lizzie wrinkled her nose. "When you have such lovely places as Westminster and the Mall?"

"Greenwich is like a little bit of the country in the city, and I am partial to it. The river is not so busy there and there is a lovely little old-world pub."

"If you say so," Lizzie sighed as she continued one knit, one pearl.

Dodo swayed in time to the hypnotic sounds of the music, imagining she was in Rupert's arms. She hoped his feelings were as deep as hers because from her vantage point she would need a very tall ladder to get out.

Standing outside the *Sainted Nun,* Dodo drew her coat tighter and checked her watch again. The weather had fallen apart since it cleared yesterday, and the wind was howling along the street as fast as the taxicabs.

"I think I have finally found a fault in the man. He is sometimes late." She scanned the street one more time. "I'm going inside," she muttered to herself and pushed open the glossy black door with its brass kick plate.

Immediately upon entering she slumped with disappointment. The place had dramatically changed…and not for the better. Rather than a charming, intimate country pub of yesteryear, it had been modernized, every available inch packed with small black tables. Hungry and thirsty patrons crowded the tight space, knee to knee. And the clientele had changed with it. She ignored a wolf whistle and went to the bar. The new barkeep had thin hair, scraped back with a vast amount of brilliantine. He squinted at her through round spectacles that perched on ruddy cheeks.

"What can I do for you, miss?" She bit back a smile. It would take a pretty sharp knife to cut through the thickness of his cockney accent.

"Do you have a menu?"

He pointed to the wall behind him where the food items were listed in chalk on a board.

"Oh!" she said. "Are you under new management?"

The short, portly man pulled on his waistcoat. "Indeed, we are, miss. Samuel Barkus at your service." He wiped his hand on a reasonably clean apron and held it out. Dodo shook his firm hand.

"Whatever happened to the previous owner?" She remembered a refined old man with thick, gray hair and sturdy, parchment menus.

"Got hit by a taxi."

Dodo's hand flew to her mouth.

Samuel Barkus shook his head. "Oh no, miss!" he cried, appearing to realize his statement had been misleading. "He broke his leg, sold up, and went to live by the coast."

44

"Thank heavens! He was a lovely old man."

"Indeed, he was," agreed Mr. Barkus.

She spotted a table becoming free on the right side and rushed to take it, waving to the new proprietor. She secured a seat and looked around. The place had lost all its charm.

With an eye on the door, she checked her watch again. Rupert was now thirty minutes late. But lack of punctuality was a fault she could live with.

The proprietor wandered over and Dodo noticed that a rather buxom woman had replaced him at the bar.

"What can I get for you, miss?"

"Nothing at present," she began not taking her eye from the door. "I'm waiting for someone."

"Let me know if you change your mind." He ran a hand over his thin hair and shimmied back to the bar.

The customers were mostly men in suits, taking a long lunch, laughing too loudly, and shouting across the tables. She would have to cross this off her list of favorite places. And she would have to apologize to Rupert when he arrived.

Dodo glanced out the window to a patio with several tables whose chairs were leaned up against them. Unfortunately, it was far too cold to eat outside. The last time she had come here was with her sister and they had eaten under a shady tree, looking across the river. Now the tree was bare and angled.

A noise from the door drew her attention back but the hope that had crested sank as an old soldier entered.

Where could Rupert be?

Her stomach grumbled but she ignored it as hunger was replaced with a slug of concern. She could not imagine Rupert would stand her up without good reason. Perhaps Beatrice had taken ill or was experiencing severe withdrawal symptoms.

She pushed the chair back and threaded her way back to the bar. The noise level had increased, and she had to shout. "Do you have a telephone?" She mimed with her hands.

The buxom woman nodded and pointed behind the bar.

"Kensington 242," she told the operator. The phone rang and rang and rang.

Something must be wrong.

She paid for the phone call and stepped outside into the windy, gloom of an English winter's day.

Where did he live? He had not given her an exact address, but she was an experienced detective. *What had he said?* A little mews in Kensington. Without looking back, she hailed a taxi.

"Kensington please!"

What had started as a small suggestion of concern sixty minutes ago had grown into a full out bellow.

"Address?" barked the cabbie, a thin man with countless stories stamped on his face.

"Uh. I don't have a specific address." The cab driver glanced over his shoulder frowning. "Are there many mews in Kensington?" She hoped her small smile telegraphed an apology.

The cabbie pushed back his cap and dragged a hand down his long, hard-scrabble face. "There are more mews in Kensington than any other place in London, I reckon."

A trolley bus passed close to them causing the taxi to swerve, narrowly missing an old man on a bicycle.

"I say, would you mind watching the road," she asked.

"Right. Let me pull over." He navigated the busy street and pulled the automobile over to the curb. "Any idea of the closest tube station?"

Dodo pursed her lips, straining to drag out a memory. "Let me see. Did he mention—yes!" She slapped her forehead. "Gloucester Road."

The cab man's face fell. "Clearly you are not familiar wiv the area," he gasped with his gravelly voice. "There are *loads* of mews near Gloucester Road Tube station, miss."

She could sense frustration building in him like a thundercloud on a blistering hot day. "I'm terribly sorry but I shall just have to canvas each one until I find it," declared Dodo. "I shall pay double your fare." Magically, the irritation was replaced with a sly smile.

"In that case…" The cabbie pulled back out into the traffic and after several miles turned into a little mews called *Holland Park*.

An old man was putting his cat out and Dodo approached him with her most engaging smile. "I say, do you happen to know if the Danforths live here?"

The man raised rheumy eyes. "I have lived here for twenty-five years and I know everyone and I can categorically state that there are no Danforths."

Retired army.

"Thank you so much." She hopped back into the cab. "Not this one."

The car wove through traffic and bicyclists and eventually turned right into a mews with a beautiful masonry arch and a sign that announced *Kynance Mews.* The small houses were immaculate and dormant trees in pots sat outside every door.

A woman was walking a small Yorkshire terrier and Dodo poked her head out of the cab window.

"Yoohoo!" Dodo cried. The woman did not turn. She tried again a little louder. "Yoohoo!" Still nothing. "Oh bother!" She slid out of the car and ran to catch up with the dogwalker, tapping her on the shoulder. The woman turned around with shock in her eyes.

"I'm terribly sorry to bother you—" The woman shook her head and pointed to her ears. Dodo raised her voice. "Do you happen to know the Danforths?"

"Darnsmiths?" repeated the woman back.

"No! DANFORTH."

The woman nodded with a smile. "Never heard of them."

Dodo's shoulders slouched. Was she ever going to find him?

"I take it he is not here," said the cabbie with a flicker of amusement.

"No." Was this just a wild goose chase?

They reversed out and soon rounded a bend before turning into yet another mews. *Cresswell Place.* It was a very tidy little road and several of the houses had orange slate on the top half and red brick on the bottom. Others were pure white on top and red on the bottom. Many also had brown ivy draping from the front. She could imagine that in the summer it was a riot of color.

Seeing no one, she approached the first door and rapped sharply. After a moment a girl in the black and white uniform of a maid answered with a question on her face.

"I'm looking for the Danforths," Dodo explained.

"Number 22," said the wisp of a girl as she closed the door.

At last!

Dodo walked to number 22 and knocked. She waited. She knocked again and leaned to the side to try to peer through a window. The interior was dark. She opened her clutch bag and withdrew a pen and notepad. She scribbled a note to Rupert and stuck it under the mat. Perhaps she had crossed paths with him. However, this conclusion did not satisfy her troubled mind. She knew enough of his manners to be convinced that he would have tried to contact her if he could.

She reached for the handle on the taxi, her heart in her boots.

"He's not here." Dodo jerked up her head to behold a woman of a certain age dressed in fuchsia chiffon from head to toe, leaning out of number 21.

"Do you happen to know where Ruper—Mr. Danforth is?" *Best not to show all one's cards.*

The woman gave her a slow once-over. "And who are you?"

"I am just a friend," she replied. "Mr. Danforth was supposed to meet me, but he never showed up. I'm worried."

The neighbor's eyes narrowed to slits. "I saw him rush out about three hours ago." She was stroking a ridiculously puffy cat.

I missed him.

Dodo turned to get back into the cab. "Thank you."

"Don't you want to know where he went?" The woman was sixty pretending to be forty.

"Do you know?" asked Dodo, taking a step back toward her.

"Yes, I overheard him. Such a lovely fellow. We are—" she dropped her voice so low Dodo had trouble hearing "—intimate friends."

Dodo stifled a choke.

"He was headed to the police station." The woman pierced her with black eyes, challenging Dodo.

"Did he say why?"

The woman ran a veined hand down the cat's silky back. "No, but I heard him tell the taxi driver and his tone was urgent. I hope everything is alright."

Dodo rushed back to the taxi who was idling his vehicle in the center of the mews. "The closest police station!" she demanded.

"Oh no, dear!" cried the cat lady after her, preening with superior knowledge. "I distinctly heard him tell the cab driver Limehouse."

Chapter 9

To say that Limehouse was squalid was not an exaggeration. Grown men slouched on the filthy curbs, tangled heads fallen against their chests. Sailors roamed the streets like ants searching for food, drink, and oblivion, and women of ill repute dotted street corners or partially hid in alleyways.

The area that had come to be known as Chinatown was not large, consisting of two interlocking streets that straddled the West India Dock. Dodo had heard tales of a notorious pub called *Charlie Brown* that was reportedly full of vice, at the center of the area. A hub of wickedness. She also knew that there were two missions in the area, an attempt to draw people away from lives of dissolution and sin.

The opium trade had begun here in Victorian times when China was in a severe trade deficit with England and had never left. It was full of opium dens where people could escape their troubles.

She looked out with serious eyes at the dregs of society and the words of the popular song *Limehouse* came to mind.

"Oh, Limehouse child
Becoming like the rest of them, wild
Poor, broken thing
But nobody's babe,
Aching and hurting you just can't behave."

As they pulled up to the insignificant police station, the formerly disgruntled cabbie turned worried eyes on Dodo. "Are you sure you'll be alright, miss? Do you want me to hang about?"

Dodo was digging in her clutch for some pound notes. "I'll be fine. I am not unused to areas like this, you might be surprised to know. Besides, I'm at the police station. I shall be safe as houses. But I thank you for your chivalry, sir."

"I am surprised. A fancy lady like you…" His head swung from left to right as he surveyed the ugly view.

"If you are concerned that I live a double life, I can assure you that I am a perfectly respectable woman. My friend must be in trouble, and I intend to help him."

She thrust the money into the cabbie's hand, stepped out of the cab and pulled down her coat to fortify her nerve.

"Thank you."

The taxi driver watched as she looked up at the little police station. It was squashed into the middle of a street full of dilapidated buildings as though a giant had pushed it into a space that was too small. The front of the building was black with soot, the gas lamps not yet lit and the black doors peeling.

She summoned a deep breath and pushed on the scruffy door.

Inside, the smell of sweat and urine was almost more than she could bear, and she dragged a hankie out of her bag to hold to her nose. Similarly slouched men lined benches on either side of a waiting area and a colorful woman in a dress that was three sizes too small and had seen better days, winked with a slanted smile that exposed black gaps in her teeth.

Dodo shuddered.

She marched to the reception desk where a young desk sergeant was bent over some paperwork. She cleared her throat.

Nothing.

She tried again.

Nothing.

"Excuse me."

The sergeant lifted his head and took a step back. "I'm sorry, miss. I didn't see you come in." His eyes slid over her expensive clothing. "What can I do for you?"

"My name is Lady Dorothea Dorchester, daughter of the Earl of Trent and I am here to inquire after a Mr. Rupert Danforth. The third."

The litany of titles quite undid the sergeant who tried to straighten his tie while smoothing his hair. "Gracious, m'lady. I...I...didn't know."

"Well, now you do," she said in a softer tone. "Is Mr. Danforth here?"

"That would be the fair-haired gentleman in the expensive suit, I suppose."

51

"Yes!" Relief grabbed her like a long-lost aunt. "So, he's here?"

"He is indeed." The sergeant hesitated, running a hand through his shocking red hair.

She could feel her temper rising. "What on earth is the matter? Can't you go and tell him I'm here?"

"Are you related to the gentleman, m'lady?"

Dodo puckered her lips with disdain. "No," she said quietly.

"Then I'm afraid—"

Before he could finish, Dodo turned her thousand-watt smile on him and he visibly wilted.

"I don't want to be the cause of you getting in trouble Sergeant...?"

"Mackay," he gulped. "Sergeant Mackay."

"Sergeant Mackay, but perhaps I could talk to your superior?" She resorted to dipping her head and batting her lashes.

The young sergeant backed up, hit the door with his heel, and turned while keeping his gaze on Dodo. "I'll be right back."

Dodo turned her back to the desk and checked her nails. The woman in the tight dress now had her arm around one of the slouching fellows. Dodo's lips pulled down of their own accord. A noise made her turn around.

"I'm Inspector Wadley." A forgettable face greeted her with a patient smile that was already slipping. "I'm sorry to have to tell you that since you are not a relative of Mr. Danforth, I cannot let you back here."

"May I ask if he has been charged with a crime?"

The inspector chuckled with no humor. "Mr. Danforth is not here as a suspect."

Dodo sucked in her cheeks. "Oh! Oh, I thought—" Time to regroup.

Think, think.

She mentally snapped her fingers. "Perhaps if I could use your phone to call Sir Matthew Cusworth?"

The inspector's head reared back. "Sir Matthew? The Commissioner?"

"That's the one."

The inspector's condescending manner fled faster than a dog on the hunt.

"I don't think there's any need to involve him, Lady Dorothea. He's a busy man. How about I just let you through and we keep it all hush hush?"

"Perfect!" she cried. "Lead the way."

The inspector opened a smoky glass door and led her down a dingy, insipid, blue hallway that had clearly not been swept since last Christmas. He stopped outside a battered door and knocked.

"Come in!"

Rupert!

Opening the door, the unremarkable inspector said, "A visitor for you, sir."

"A visitor?"

Dodo pushed past the officious policeman.

"Dodo!" Rupert's tone was one part shock two parts horror. "What are you doing here?"

"I used my detecting skills to find you when you stood me up." She stood smiling awkwardly at his apparent discomfort. "What on earth has happened?"

Rupert slapped his head. "Lunch! I completely forgot! Can you forgive me?"

Inspector Wadley closed the door to the box like room and Rupert let her sit in the spindly chair. He clasped his hands together and sighed. "I really don't want to drag you into all this." His eyes were brim full of pain.

"Why don't you tell me all about it and let me decide?" she assured him.

His expression was tortured. "My sister, Beatrice, has been arrested for murder."

Whatever scenario she had unconsciously concocted this was not it.

"Arrested? For murder?"

Rupert began to pace. "It's all my fault."

Dodo was confused. "Perhaps if you start at the beginning."

"I let myself get distracted by you. I should not have neglected Beatrice. I didn't check on her after our date yesterday, assuming that she was asleep and went to bed with no great concerns,

53

thinking about our lunch in Greenwich and awoke this morning with great anticipation." He ran his hands roughly through his hair.

"I do not keep a valet," he continued, "and had a late breakfast. I was shaving in preparation for meeting you when the telephone rang. I picked it up expecting to hear your voice and instead heard the less than dulcet tones of P.C. Plod telling me that they were holding my sister on suspicion of murder.

I assured him that she was asleep upstairs, but he insisted that he hold while I checked.

She was not there."

His face was a study in misery and Dodo's impulse was to kiss it from his face.

"All other thoughts fled, and I rushed over here," he said. "I should have called you. I'm so sorry."

Dodo jumped up and put her hand on his arm. "Rupert, think nothing of it." Then she began to pace too, suddenly all business. "Who is she accused of killing?"

"This is where it becomes extremely bizarre," he said, grabbing his neck. "They think she killed the woman in the papers. The woman you had the meeting with—Stella Stanhope."

The world tilted on its axis and Dodo sank onto the rickety chair. "Stella!"

"Yes. They haven't actually let me see Beatrice yet, so I only know what the police have told me."

"Which is what exactly?"

"Not much." Waves of anguish rolled across his features. "I should have checked on her last night. If I had, this could all have been avoided. I would have known she was struggling and helped her through the worst of it. It appears that she left while I was out with you and came to Limehouse to seek the services of an opium den."

"Oh Rupert! How bally awful!"

"Just when I thought she was doing better," he gasped. "Addiction is the very devil." He looked up, his face as tortured as the Virtuous Pagans in Dante's first circle of hell.

It was too much to bear and she almost surrendered to empathy for this strong man who was crumbling before her, but her inner sleuth took control. Rupert needed her to be strong. She needed to be armed with the facts.

"Then what happened?"

"She took a taxi here, found a place and availed herself of the paraphernalia, selected a mattress and lay in oblivion for most of the afternoon. The police got a tip about the murder weapon and searched all the dens in the area until they found a bloody knife stuffed down under the mattress Beatrice was laying on." He motioned with his hands. "You can imagine the excitement that generated. And to make things worse it matched the type of weapon used to kill Stella. They dragged my comatose sister to the police station and have put her in a cell to sleep it off."

"Well, though it sounds pretty damning, it is only circumstantial evidence," declared Dodo. "What possible motive can she have? Does she even know Stella?"

"No! I don't know." He dragged his hands down his face. "My brain is frazzled, and I've not been able to think straight. But I know one thing— there is no way my sister killed anyone. Oh, Dodo, do you think we can get her out of here?"

Dodo puffed air as she considered their options. Could they get her released on bail?

Chief Inspector Blood might be able to help, though the thought of asking him made her cringe.

"Let me call in some favors at Scotland Yard," she said, glancing at her watch. It was now almost six o' clock.

Rupert nodded and she walked down the hall, nerves jangling, and returned to the desk sergeant.

"May I use your phone?"

"Are you going to call Sir Matthew Cusworth?" he asked in a small voice.

"No. Just Scotland Yard. I have some friends over there."

Sergeant Mackay swallowed hard and handed her the phone.

Her fingers trembled as she held the receiver. "Scotland Yard."

"Putting you through."

When the Scotland Yard receptionist answered, Dodo almost hung up as her courage faltered. Things had been left

55

so…unfinished between them. What if Blood refused to even take her call?

But Rupert needed her.

"Chief Inspector Blood, please." She held her breath. There was no going back now.

"I'm afraid he's on assignment in the North," the receptionist replied.

Dodo exhaled with relief and disappointment.

"Can I put you through to someone else?" asked the receptionist.

There was no one else to turn to. "No, thank you," she said and replaced the phone quickly with a tight stomach.

"We had a man from Scotland Yard here earlier," Sergeant Mackay said. "An Inspector Anderson. He's the one the top brass assigned to the case. He took the knife and matched it to the deceased's injuries. I s'pect he'll be back shortly. Don't know regular hours those detectives."

Well, that would have been useful to know!

"Is that so?" she said, shifting her irritation at the man like a mother might shift her baby to the other hip. It was time for a more determined attempt at persuasion. She lowered her face and gazed at the sergeant out of the corner of her eyes. Scarlet crept up his neck like a rash, to meet the roots of his red hair. "Couldn't you let Mr. Danforth at least see his sister?" she pleaded.

The sergeant took a step back. "I don't have that kind of authority, m'lady. You'll have to talk to Inspector Wadley again."

"And where can I find him?" She kept her tone light.

"Room 5. All the way down the hall."

Dodo threw off the lady-in-distress mask and marched back down the way she had come and knocked firmly on the door of room 5.

"Come in!" The inspector pushed his lips up to his nose in distress. "Oh, it's you."

Sugar or vinegar?

She had a fifty-fifty chance of success. She sat on the chair in front of his desk and balanced the clutch purse on her knees.

"We seem to have got off on the wrong foot," she began. "I am only trying to help. I was just wondering why Mr. Danforth has not been able to see his sister?"

The bland inspector screwed up his raisin color eyes. "That would be because she is in no condition to talk. She's still under the influence of the opium."

"And other than finding a knife—"

"A bloody knife," the inspector corrected.

"Indeed, a bloody knife, under the mattress where Miss Danforth was reposing, what other evidence do you have to tie her to the crime?"

Inspector Wadley scrunched his chin with his hand and examined Dodo. "Nothing...yet."

"I am sure you are aware that the crime was committed two days ago, and multiple people could have used that particular mattress since that time?"

The inspector's lips tightened, and his nostrils flared. "That is so. But the Chinese gentleman that owns the opium den said that the mattress had not been used by anyone else since the crime."

Dodo scowled. "And is he a credible witness? An honest man?"

The inspector withdrew like a turtle into its shell. "Uh, no."

The temptation to jump on this information was strong but Dodo knew she was walking a tightrope. "Then may I suggest that you release Miss Danforth into the custody of her brother until you have a stronger case against her, so that she may recover at home? I give my word that we will cooperate with the authorities, and we will not allow her to flee. She will return for questioning as soon as she is coherent. Or better still, you could question her at the house."

Inspector Wadley narrowed his eyes, fingering his mustache.

"You can call Sir Matthew Cusworth for a character witness, if you like," said Dodo.

That seemed to tip the scales as the inspector blanched at mention of the head of the metropolitan police force.

"I shall have to run it by Inspector Anderson at Scotland Yard."

"Of course." She smiled as sweetly as a nun on Sunday.

He picked up the black utilitarian telephone that sat on his desk and waited.

"I shall just go back to tell the good news to Mr. Danforth," Dodo said.

She hurried back down the hall and burst through the door. "Rupert, I think they are going to let Beatrice go."

His expression changed from that of a drowning man to one who had been thrown a life ring. "You marvelous, marvelous woman!" he cried, throwing his arms around her.

"I think you had better save your affirmations," she said, pulling away slightly. "She is still a suspect, they are merely releasing her into your custody until they can question her."

"It's more than I could have asked for at this point," he said, kissing her cheek. "How on earth did you manage it?"

"You just have to know how to deal with the police," she said. "They are checking with Scotland Yard right now."

The door opened and Inspector Wadley held out some paperwork. Rupert grabbed it and signed.

"Seems you are quite well known at HQ, Lady Dorothea," he said with reluctant admiration.

"I may have done a few things with the department," she said, straightening her hat.

The inspector held out a short arm. "Let me take you to Miss Danforth."

Rupert grabbed Dodo's hand and they followed him down the stairs and into the dark cellar. It was lit with one bare lightbulb that hardly made a dent. The floors were dirty and the air stale. When they approached the cell, Rupert let out a sharp cry. His sister was laying on a hard wooden bench, her light brown hair hanging almost to the nasty floor, dead to the world and wrapped in a rough blanket. As the key turned in the lock and the door screeched on its hinges she stirred, eyes squinting in confusion.

"Rupert?" She brought to mind an unearthed mole. "Where am I?"

He went to her and held her slight frame in his arms as though she were a rag doll.

"I am here to take you home, darling."

"What is this place?" She looked around the mean space, wrinkling her nose.

His eyes met Dodo's.

"You are in jail. They think you murdered someone."

Chapter 10

A droopy Beatrice was now settled on the brown leather sofa in Rupert's little mews house. Purple shadows underscored her large, sad eyes as she looked up at her older brother. He dropped to the floor beside her.

"I'm so sorry Rupert," she said, her gray eyes shining. "The craving was just too strong and before I knew it, I found myself in Limehouse. Someone told me of an opium den that was higher class, but I was so desperate I walked into the first one I saw.

"Have you done that before?" he asked.

She raised her face full of shame and guilt. "Never. There is a man…he supplies my needs but I couldn't get hold of him." She gripped Rupert's hand. "That stuff has me in its grip. I am no longer free." A sob erupted. "I am ruined."

Rupert put an arm around her while Dodo sat in a neat club chair next to an arched, brick fireplace. Maps and pictures of tall ships hung from the walls reminding her of the library at Blackwood, her cousins' estate, where she had spent so much time as a child.

The fire had burned down causing the air to chill and Dodo took full advantage of a thick, wool blanket slung across the back of her chair. She watched with interest as Rupert gently tended to his sister and fell a little further in love. No mention of the arrest had yet been made but the detective in her was bursting to interview Beatrice and begin her own investigation.

Rupert threw another log from a brass bucket on to the embers and taking the fire poker, churned up the ashes. Beatrice diminished without him close, shrinking into the sofa, fragile and broken. Though gaunt at present, it was obvious that she had been an attractive girl, with long legs and thick, full hair. It was a crime that she had ever been seduced by the awful drug.

Rupert stood with his back to the flames, hands behind him, a grave expression overshadowing his chiseled features.

"Bea, do you understand why you were at the police station?"

Her face crumpled like a child who has been reprimanded by a favorite aunt. "I can't remember. It's all very foggy."

Rupert shared a glance with Dodo then plowed on. "Do you remember me telling you that the police believe you killed someone."

Her tired eyes filled with confusion at the suggestion. It was obvious that Beatrice had forgotten and could not process the meaning of his words.

"Why would anyone think that? What possible reason would I have to kill anyone?" She pulled the soft blanket covering her, up to her ears as if the blanket could form a barrier of protection from the frightening scenario.

"One of the reasons is because they found a bloody knife next to you on the mattress. They believe it is the knife used to kill someone. It's called circumstantial evidence. It connects you to the crime," said Rupert.

"What?" she gasped.

Beatrice's misty eyes trailed over to Dodo with a question. "Who are you again? I know you told me, but I can't remember."

"This is Dodo." Rupert explained turning his head to smile at her. "My girlfriend."

Her heart skipped a beat. This was the first time he had referred to her as that. When they had bundled Beatrice out of the station and into a taxi, he had simply introduced her by name.

"Dodo is also an experienced detective. I hope she can help us sort this thing out before it goes any further as it is obviously a huge mistake."

Beatrice wiped her eyes on her sleeve. "You said 'one' of the things. What are the others?"

"Well, you were found in the location where the murder took place," explained Dodo.

"I don't know anything about a murder. I've been a bit out of it in case they hadn't noticed. Who was killed?"

"A woman called Stella Stanhope." Dodo watched the tired eyes for signs of recognition. None. Instead, Beatrice's brows knit together in confusion.

"Who is she?"

The log popped in the fireplace.

"An important career woman in the fashion industry," said Dodo.

"Sadly, if she were just one of the working women of Limehouse it probably wouldn't have made the newspapers," said Rupert.

Dodo nodded in agreement. "So, you have never heard of her, Beatrice?"

"No, never." Rupert's sister was picking at the blanket with two agitated fingers.

"Alright. Let's try and piece together what we do know before you have to give a statement." Dodo shifted forward in the chair. "Rupert left yesterday, Tuesday, late in the morning and thought you were still asleep in bed. Were you?"

The struggle to remember was plain on her face, her gaze passing through Dodo as if she was a specter. "Yesterday..." She tried to run a hand through her thick hair, but it was a tangled mess. The hand dropped to her lap, then her eyes snapped wide open. "Yes. The pink lady next door was calling to her cat and woke me up. I looked at the clock and it was around noon."

Dodo clapped her hands. "Very good. Then what happened?"

"I was awfully hungry and went to the larder in search of food...and you." She stared at her brother.

"I left you a note on the counter, explaining where I was and that I would be back."

"I didn't see it." She looked ready to burst into tears again. She was as fragile as a dried flower found between the pages of an old book.

Time to bring things back to the matter at hand. "You were searching for food," prompted Dodo. "Then what happened? Did you find any?"

"Nothing tempting..." Her face lit up as a memory surfaced. "Now I remember. There's a wonderful bakery around the corner so I found some money and popped out to get a bun." Pride at recalling that important fact energized Beatrice and Dodo got a glimpse of the girl she had been before the devil's potion poisoned her spirit. And here was something they could easily check. Someone would have seen her, waited on her.

"According to the papers the murder occurred during the night, early Tuesday morning," said Dodo, thinking out loud. "Rupert, you did not check on Beatrice Monday night after she went to bed and assumed she was still asleep when you left Tuesday for the National Gallery."

"That is correct," he said.

No one to corroborate that she was in bed at the time of the murder.

"And upon your return, since the house was quiet and she was not downstairs, you did not disturb her when you arrived back on Tuesday."

"I thought sleep was better than withdrawal symptoms."

"Then as you were dressing for the day, Wednesday morning, you were called by the police station to inform you that Beatrice had been arrested."

"That's about the long and short of it," he responded.

Dodo searched in her bag for her notebook and dug out a pencil. "Let's think of things that point to Beatrice's innocence," she began. "Where was Beatrice at the time of the murder? If we can provide her with an alibi their case falls apart. Rupert, could she have left the house that night without you hearing?"

"What time was the murder committed?"

Dodo reached for the newspaper that was on the coffee table and scanned the latest article.

"It says between one and two in the morning."

"I was definitely home," said Rupert. "But I didn't hear anything. I'm a pretty heavy sleeper so I don't know that I'm any help there." She could feel his disappointment from across the room.

"If Beatrice had gone to Limehouse on Monday night, it would have been to get a fix. We can ask the opium den operators if she came twice."

"I didn't," Beatrice said. "I had never been there before yesterday."

"Unfortunately, you are not a credible witness," said Dodo softly. "You are an unreliable source because you are unconscious at times. What we need to do is ask around. If no one saw you there Monday night, that will help."

The room had got steadily darker as they sat round the fire and Rupert stood to turn on the light.

"Let's talk about the bakery. You were definitely in Kensington Wednesday afternoon. We can check that." She chewed the pencil. "For argument's sake let's say you did kill Stella—"

Beatrice cried out. "I wouldn't!"

"I know, but we have to think dispassionately like the police. A person in your condition would not think things through like a sober person. If you killed Stella, you would have blood on your clothes. We should check the laundry hamper—unless it has gone to the cleaner's already?"

"No, not till Monday."

"Well, that's a relief. We'll check after we've done theorizing." She tapped the pencil on the edge of the notebook. "What happened after you went to the bakery?" she prodded. "Did you come home?"

Bea's head dropped back. After several minutes of concentration she said, "I finished my bun walking along the street— Mummy would have been furious. But the food didn't satisfy the craving as I'd hoped, and a wave of longing and anxiety hit me so strong I could hardly stand up. I felt sick and dizzy. I looked around in desperation and saw a taxi. I knew about Limehouse and asked to be taken there. I was sweating and trembling in the taxi and as soon as he stopped, I threw him some money and went into the first den I saw. When you are that frantic you don't care about the usual things like cleanliness and the right sort of people. I saw a man, with a long, black plait down his back wearing traditional Chinese clothing and said I needed a fix. He nodded to a girl who showed me to the bed and gave me the stuff. Honestly, that was the last I remember until you woke me up at the station."

Would they be able to find the taxi driver who dropped her off? It was doubtful—needle in a haystack—but the Chinese man was certainly someone they could question.

"Do you remember anyone approaching you while you were—" Dodo hesitated. How was one to talk about the experience brought about by the drug?

64

Beatrice solved the problem. "When you are under the influence, you're in a different world. It is like a dream and anyone in the real world would just become part of that dream."

Dodo had a thought. "Did they take your fingerprints at the station?"

Beatrice looked down at her hands and turned them over. Telltale smudges of ink residue indicated that they had.

"Good!" declared Dodo. "Hopefully they will not find your prints on the knife and your status will change from suspect to witness."

Dodo had heard that hell was a place where regrets lived with you eternally causing untold mental anguish. Such was the current expression on the poor girl's face.

Dodo turned in the chair to face Rupert whose mien mirrored his sister's. "I think it is time to bring Lizzie here so that you and I can start investigating." Clearly the girl could not be left alone. "What do you think?"

"I want to do *something*," he said.

"The first thing we need to do is question the people at the opium den. I don't know how helpful they will be given that their business is conducted in the shadows but it's a start." She stood. "May I use your telephone?"

Rupert led her to the hall, pointing to a pedestal instrument. He squeezed her hand and returned to the sitting room.

After the operator put her through to the hidey hole, she summarized the situation for Lizzie and asked her if she would mind tending to the patient.

"Oh, that is terrible stuff, that is. My uncle Morton got addicted to the stuff after he got gout and took it for the pain. Became a shell of a man. Robbed him of his dignity. Tore my dad apart. You can count on me, m'lady. Just give me the address and I will be there in a jiffy." For the thousandth time Dodo thanked heaven for the girl who was so much more than a maid. She gave her the address and replaced the receiver.

Time to tackle the laundry. She mounted the narrow stairs and was faced with just three doors. She pushed the first one open and looked inside. The color palette was all browns, and the bed was made with precision. The woodsy fragrance coming from the dressing table was the final clue to this being Rupert's room. Curious, she stepped in. Though the space was plain everything was of the highest quality and the most beautiful oil painting of a horse hung over the heavy oak bed. A small copy of the New Testament was on the bedside table along with a crystal decanter of water and a chunky glass. Though she wanted to stay and find out more about the man she was falling in love with, she had a job to do.

She withdrew.

After finding the tiny bathroom, she went to the third door. This room was in utter confusion, sheets rumpled, coverlet hanging off the bedframe, and pillows tossed around the floor. She spotted a wicker hamper in the corner, but it was almost empty. Clothes were scattered hither and yon, and she gingerly began the task of retrieving them for inspection. After ten minutes she felt satisfied that she had examined every article of laundry in the room.

No blood.

"Lizzie is on her way to the rescue," she said when she re-entered the sitting room, addressing her comments to Rupert who summoned up a weak smile of appreciation. She turned to Beatrice. "Would you like some tea?"

Rupert's sister nodded. "I'm parched now that I think about it."

"I am not the world's best tea maker." Dodo's lips curled into a smile. "*She* is on her way. But I think I make a decent cup."

"I'll show you where everything is," said Rupert and they both walked through to the kitchen.

It was mostly modern but with older touches of hooks and brass on the walls, and Dodo realized that it had been a kind of tackle room in its heyday. Either Rupert or his uncle must have re-fitted the room and it had been done with taste and efficiency in mind.

"You don't have a housekeeper?" she asked him.

"It's just me most of the time. I dine out or at my father's club. Someone comes once a week to clean and take my clothes to the laundry. I live a simple life."

"Does that simple life include a kettle?" Dodo was searching the stove top to no avail.

"I have an electric one," said Rupert pointing to a corner of the kitchen.

Although electric kettles had been around for decades, Dodo eyed it with suspicion. The cook at her parent's house, would rather die than use new appliances, and Dodo wasn't sure that in this case she would not be proven correct. Would water boiled by electricity make the tea taste different? She took it to the sink and filled it with water. The kitchen had a plated glass window, and she could just make out a small garden with some chairs and benches under a flower arbor which was brown and uninviting at this time of year.

After plugging the kettle in she asked for a tea pot. "I actually don't drink much tea when it's just me," Rupert confessed.

"But you have some?"

"Of course."

He routed around in a larder and came out with a tea tin that was at least a hundred years old. "It was my uncle's," he said, answering her unasked question. "I think it went with him to several battlefields."

The making of tea was so ordinary, so domesticated, that for a short moment she was able to forget that his sister had been implicated in a murder and was, in fact, desperately ill with her addiction.

She added two heaping spoonfuls of the fragrant leaves to the bottom of the pot. When the water was ready, she poured a little over the leaves and replaced the lid.

Rupert raised his brows. "I'm impressed that you know how, to be honest. You don't seem the domesticated type."

"I'm not really," she said as she swirled the pot around, "but I loved going down to the kitchens as a child—I was always hungry— and I watched the professionals do it on so many occasions that I kind of learned. Not that I do it very often because Lizzie makes the best cup of tea in the world."

She opened the lid again and inhaled the scent of the wet tea and satisfied, filled the rest of the pot. "You will be happy to know there are no bloody clothes in Beatrice's room. I hope you don't mind me taking the liberty?"

"Of course not! That is a relief." He slipped his arms around her waist and breathed into her neck. "What would I do without you?"

Dodo placed the lid on the teapot and said, "Now we just need to let it steep for a while. Do you have a tea cosy?"

Rupert snorted. "No, I do not."

Dodo couldn't help a half smile at his indignation. "How about a tea towel? That will do."

He lifted a finger. "I do have some of those." He went to a drawer near the sink and opened it and then stepped back as if he had been stung.

"Whatever is the matter?"

He pulled a towel out, holding the end between two fingers. "This!"

It was covered in dried blood.

Chapter 11

If the towel had been a rattle snake Rupert could not have dropped it any quicker. He backed away in horror.

Dodo grabbed a spoon and poked the towel. There was blood in the middle, consistent with someone wiping their hands…or a knife.

She took a breath. "Let's not jump to conclusions. There could be a perfectly innocent explanation for this."

"You don't really believe that." He stared at her, panic flashing in his eyes. "I believed implicitly in my sister's innocence but now…"

"It is a little setback to be sure, and we will have to take it to the police as evidence—"

"Surely not! Can't we wait for them to find it?"

"Rupert, there is something you need to know about me. I cherish integrity. I cannot in good conscience withhold this from the police. I am not saying we have to take it immediately. I think we can do a little investigating in Limehouse and then present it."

"No! This will hang my sister! Can't you make an exception?"

Dodo bit her cheek and narrowed her eyes. "Rupert, you're not thinking straight. I know she is your sister, but you have to trust the system. It could be blood from a steak, or someone may have caught themselves on something. If we conceal a piece of evidence, we could be charged with aiding and abetting."

He backed away from Dodo. "I thought you were on our side."

She clenched her teeth. "I'm on the side of truth."

"So, you believe she is guilty?" The usual calm, smooth voice had jumped half an octave and his jaw was strained with fear.

"No, but I think *you* think she could be guilty." She stared hard, challenging him to deny it.

For a moment he returned her glare, eyes fighting hysteria.

This relationship might end before it has really begun.

His face crumpled and he dropped his head into his hands in defeat.

Dodo breathed again.

"You're right," he moaned. "I do. I know that strung out people can behave in ways they never would when sober, and let's face it, she did shoplift a few weeks ago. I was desperate to keep that from my parents but this…this is so much worse." He sank onto a wooden stool.

Dodo placed her hands on his shoulders. "I do not believe she did this."

Rupert clasped one of her hands. "Thank you."

"Let us go where the evidence leads," she continued. "You will have to be brave with your sister's future at stake, but you must try to dial back your emotions."

He shifted on the stool. "I hate the idea, but I can see that you are right."

"Let's find a bag for this towel and take it to the police. They will be able to run tests to determine whether this is human or animal blood. Keep the faith until we know."

"They can do that?"

"Yes. In 1901 the Germans created such a test. I was interested and found a book at the library. It was fascinating. They can even compare blood at the scene of a murder to the victim and see if it's a match."

"You never cease to amaze me. You are unexpected in so many ways." He took her hand and pulled her to him. She leaned her head against his chest, relieved that the explosive moment that could have divided them was over.

"Should we ask her about it?" asked Rupert.

"I doubt that Beatrice would have any memory of it even if she did use it to wipe up blood, and it will just serve to worry her more at this point. Let's wait for the testing to be done and if it *is* human blood then we can address the matter with her. Do you think you can handle going back in there and acting naturally?"

He covered his eyes with both hands. "I don't know, honestly. Dodo, you have nerves of steel. How do you do it?"

She smirked. "Well, for one thing she is not my sister and for another, I have done this quite a few times, now. I trust the evidence and the process."

A sharp knock sent them both jumping.

"That must be Lizzie. That was quick even for her."

She left Rupert in the kitchen and went to the door but when she pulled it open the lady in fuchsia was there, sans cat.

"Oh!" She peered around Dodo, her penciled brows disappearing into her dyed hairline. "I was wondering if Mr. Danforth had any sugar?"

"I'd have to ask him." Dodo's fingers itched to slam the door. The woman's timing could not have been worse.

The neighbor grasped a garish pendant that hung from her wrinkled neck. "He is home then?"

"Yes, but…" Dodo tried to think of an excuse off the top of her head that would send the woman packing. Blank, she told the truth. "He's just had some bad news, so it's not a good time."

The woman's hand came up to fluff her hair. "That's too bad. Perhaps talking to someone older would help." She laid emphasis on the word 'older'.

Really?

"I'll let him know you offered," she said closing the door on the inquisitive neighbor.

She checked on Beatrice before rushing back to the kitchen. She was laying on the sofa, sound asleep.

"Where's Lizzie?" asked Rupert.

"It wasn't her. It was your over-friendly neighbor."

Comprehension dawned. "Mrs. Prescott. Yes, she is very eager. She has been widowed for five years. I have to sneak out to avoid her, sometimes. I think she does nothing but watch my house."

"That could be useful," mused Dodo, considering the widow in a new light. "Nosy neighbors can make great witnesses. If we're lucky, she may have seen Beatrice leave for the bakery. I'll have Lizzie strike up a conversation with her. Now, as soon as she gets here, we need to get over to Limehouse and find out just what happened after your sister got there."

Dodo lifted the lid to the pot again and satisfied, placed the pot on a tray after asking where the cups and saucers were.

Rupert roused Beatrice who was still dozing and offered her some tea. He took a cup himself, but Dodo noticed he did not take one sip. In contrast, Dodo let the warm, sweet liquid soothe her. There was no denying the situation was tricky.

Another knock on the door stirred Dodo from her maudlin thoughts. "That will be Lizzie."

When she opened the door and saw her faithful friend, she wrapped her in a big hug. As close as they were for a maid and her mistress, Lizzie pushed back, surprised.

"M'lady, I have never seen you so rattled." Lizzie pulled Dodo in close, and Dodo sank into her maid's dependable frame.

"I don't think I've ever been so emotionally close to a crime before," she explained. "The man I love is suffering and it's almost too much to bear. I'm afraid of the truth," she confessed. She let go, producing a stiff smile and showed Lizzie in.

"What a lovely little place this is," said Lizzie looking around the narrow hall with its horse paraphernalia and hunting pictures. Dodo led her through to the sitting room and right before pushing through the door said, "Rupert has a snoopy neighbor on that side." She indicated with her head. "I need to know if she saw anything unusual early Tuesday morning or anytime today. I'll leave that investigation to you."

"Of course."

"Rupert and I will leave now that you are here. Keep a sharp eye on Beatrice. She is apparently prone to wander."

She pushed on through to the sitting room, face bright. "Here's Lizzie."

Rupert reached for Lizzie's hand and shook it warmly. They had met at Blackwood Manor. "You are very welcome, Lizzie! Thank you so much." He looked at Beatrice who had dropped off again. "Should I wake her?"

"Perhaps that would be a good idea since I'm a stranger to her, sir," said Lizzie.

He gently shook his sister who struggled to open her eyes, squinting into the dim light and blinking rapidly.

"Bea, this is Dodo's maid, Lizzie. I have to leave but she will stay with you."

The bleary eyes slid over to Lizzie and stopped. Bea made a slight nod and closed her eyes again. "I am so tired."

"Of course. I'll be back later." He kissed the top of her matted head.

"Mmm," was the only reply.

"I've got her," assured Lizzie. "Off you go."

Dodo grabbed her coat and Rupert pulled a jacket from a small cupboard in the hall that was full of rubber boots, scarves, and coats.

"Ready?" she said.

"As I'll ever be," he replied.

Hopeful stars graced the velvet sky as they waited in the dark for a taxi, their breath forming plumes of steam that mingled in the cold night air. The wind had dropped along with the temperature. Rupert fastened his arm securely around Dodo, and she leaned into him, belonging.

"There's one." He released her, stepping forward to flag it down.

"Limehouse," he told the driver when they were settled.

The rough man, whose face bore scars of street fights, looked over his shoulder at them, frowning. "Are you sure, guv'nor? Not really the place for a lady at this hour."

"We're sure," affirmed Dodo.

"If you say so!" The driver pulled out into the traffic and trundled along the busy streets of the capital city. People with no worries were walking along, carefree and light-hearted, and Dodo envied them.

"You need to be careful, there was a murder in Limehouse on Monday," continued the driver. "Last headline I saw said they had arrested someone, though. A girl, I think. Posh, like you."

Rupert blanched.

"Did they put the suspect's name?" Dodo asked, on the edge of her seat, staring into Rupert's worried face.

"No. Just said she was a person of interest." He roughly rubbed his bulbous nose.

The solace of relief hugged them, but Dodo knew it was only a matter of time.

As the journey continued, the buildings became less well tended. Fewer cars peppered the streets and shadowy figures hung in backstreets.

"Address?" asked the cabbie.

Rupert gave the name of the opium den.

"Ah," said the driver, the expression dripping with innuendo. "I see how it is."

"But—" began Rupert.

Dodo grabbed his arm and shook her head. "The less people know the better."

Within minutes the car slowed and pulled over. Rupert shoved some money into the driver's hand and slammed the door. Dodo turned to look at the dingy den. The building was indistinguishable from its neighbors except for the delicate Chinese woman dressed in red silk who beckoned to them from inside.

Speaking no words, she opened the door as they approached, unleashing a cloud of the potent ammonia type odor. Dodo put a handkerchief to her mouth and suppressed the urge to cough.

The inside of the establishment was dark, with low gas lights casting eerie shadows along the grimy walls. A reception desk, like in any hostelry, faced the door and another, pretty, young Chinese girl greeted them with a bow and a smile. Dodo imagined that if Hades ran an hotel, it would look a lot like this.

"Two?" the girl asked.

"No," began Rupert, holding his palm up. "We would like to talk to the owner."

The girl's head tipped to the side and the beautiful almond eyes narrowed. "Owner?" The thickness of her accent betrayed that she did not speak much English. At least, that was the impression she wanted to send.

"Perhaps describe him with hand actions," whispered Dodo.

Rupert pantomimed a man with a long braid and the suspicious dark eyes lit up. "Ah Lin!" she declared and then shook her head rapidly with eyes closed and lips thinned.

Rupert sniffed with exasperation.

Dodo withdrew some money from her clutch and extended it toward the girl. Her eyes locked on it like a hunter on its prey, but she did not reach for the cash. Instead, she bowed and disappeared.

"Do we wait?" asked Rupert, tapping the shabby desk with nervous fingers.

"Yes. We must wait. He undoubtedly has a spy hole through which to examine us. Try not to look anxious. If he thinks we are here for business, he may come out."

Ten minutes passed and Dodo began to think her gamble had failed. She was about to admit defeat when a middle-aged Chinese man with a long braid and a black cap appeared, as if by magic, behind the desk.

"I am Ah Lin." His accent was as broad as the girls', but there was something artificial and forced about his pronunciation. He was laying it on thick for their benefit.

Rupert extended a hand, but the Chinese man merely looked at it. Rupert let it hang awkwardly at his side.

"Good evening, sir." Rupert began.

The proprietor simply stared.

"You are the owner of this establishment, I understand."

A statue could have produced more emotion.

Rupert cut worried eyes over to Dodo who nodded encouragement. "I am interested in a girl who came here yesterday and was removed by the police."

The impenetrable eyes snapped over to Dodo and back to Rupert with the hint of an ugly smile. "A girl?"

"She is my sister," clarified Rupert.

Ah Lin nodded. "Sister. Yes." He strung the last word out as his fingers slid down his long mustache.

Dots of color stained Rupert's cheeks. "No really. She is my sister. She was taken by the police from here."

Stone-faced, lips barely moving, Ah Lin said, "Police. I remember. No good for business." He turned to leave and Rupert reached out and caught his arm. The Chinese man glared at Rupert's hand with disdain and shrugged it off.

"I'm sorry," said Rupert, wiping his mouth with a sleeve. "Please sir, she was found with a knife beside her. Do you know anything about it?" His hands described the blade of a knife.

Ah Lin placed his palms together and bowed. "Ah yes, knife. Big knife. Lot of blood."

Rupert jumped on this. "Did she arrive with the knife?"

Ah Lin wagged a finger. "Respect my customer's privacy," he purred. "I have reputation."

"I must know," Rupert begged. "The police think she killed someone."

The dark brows on Ah Lin's inscrutable face knitted together. "This respectable place. No murders."

Dodo could feel frustration rising like high tide. The man was as impervious to mercy as a brick wall.

Before she could stop him, Rupert leaned over the counter and grabbed the little man's tunic. "You little—" Immediately, two heavy set Chinese men seeped from the walls. Rupert towered over them by several inches, but they had him on mass.

Rupert released Ah Lin.

The Chinese proprietor smoothed his shirt and sharpened his stare. "You go. Now!"

Rupert hesitated and the guards took a step forward.

"I think we've exhausted this line of investigation," said Dodo, her head high and her tone crisp and clear. "Let's go, darling."

She touched Rupert's arm and his shoulders dropped, breaking the spell of wrath that held him bound.

"Let's go!" she repeated.

Rupert tore his angry eyes from Ah Lin and allowed Dodo to take his arm and lead him from the building. She could feel him trembling.

Out in the crisp, biting cold, Rupert deflated. "I ruined it! Idiot!"

"He wasn't going to tell you anything," said Dodo squeezing his arm. "I've met the type before. He enjoys the power it gives him over others. No, we will have to send in a spy."

"A spy?" cried Rupert in astonishment. "You mean someone pretending to be a customer?"

"Yes, going in 'undercover' the police call it."

"Let me. I can do it."

Dodo snickered as a sailor walked by, a woman on each arm. "There is no disguise I could create that would get you back in there," she explained. "That bridge is in ashes, darling. And I can't do it either, I would be recognized."

"Then who?" asked Rupert as they lingered across the street.

"It needs to be someone Ah Lin has never met." She snapped her fingers. "Lizzie!"

Rupert snorted. "Will she do it?"

"If you are very nice to her—she has a soft spot for you."

"Does she?" His surprise was endearing. So often the beautiful were arrogant and cocksure.

"Yes. She liked you before I did."

He scratched his eyebrow and an easy grin spread across his features." Then let's go and ask her."

"No, first we must take the towel to the station. We must show them we are willing to share information even when it is damaging to our cause, and in my experience, they will be more willing to share information with us."

Rupert groaned. "They will arrest Bea again."

"I'd say there is a fifty-fifty chance. Either they will wait to test whether the blood is human, or they will arrest her right away."

One of the enormous bodyguards exited the den and stood, arms crossed, staring.

"Time to go!" cried Dodo, pulling Rupert down the street toward the police station.

Chapter 12

As they walked to the police station a clock struck eight. The cold bled into Dodo's joints and she clung tight to Rupert's arm as stray dogs loped by and drunken songs behind closed doors penetrated the quiet.

When they pushed into the welcome light of the police station, Dodo saw that the desk sergeant was not the same person as on their last visit. He was older with jowls that drooped like a bloodhound. The deep lines of his brow rose in arcs as they approached the desk and Dodo realized that upper class people rarely, if ever, crossed this threshold.

Rupert was still shaken from the encounter with Ah Lin, and Dodo thought it best if she took the lead on this occasion.

"What can I do for you fine people," asked the sergeant, pen to the ready. His voice was much higher than his person suggested.

"My name is Lady Dorothea Dorchester and I need to see Inspector Wadley."

The pencil dropped from his fingers. "May I ask the nature of your interest?"

"This is Mr. Rupert Danforth, the brother of the suspect in the murder in Limehouse, and we have found some evidence that may be of interest to the case."

By the look of shock on his face Dodo concluded that he had expected some report of personal robbery.

"The murder? Yes indeed. Let me find him for you. I don't believe he has gone home yet." He left the desk, passing through a frosted glass door.

Remorse and self-recrimination were stamped all over Rupert's features. "I can't believe how badly I messed that up." He was clearly referring to their interview with the ominous Ah Lin.

"Of the many things I have learned from my sleuthing, one is that things rarely go off smoothly," she said. "We tried. We failed. We must learn from our failure and try again."

"You really are remarkable, you know. I can honestly say I've never met a woman quite like you."

"Mr. Danforth?" Inspector Wadley appeared behind the desk with the sergeant. His face was as forgettable as ever. "You have information, I gather. Please, follow me."

As she remembered, the inspector's office was small and cramped but tidy. Piles of pages were stacked with precision on either side of his blotting pad.

He steepled his fingers. "Now then, what can you tell me?"

Dodo nodded to Rupert. "I found something in my kitchen drawer that could be interpreted as rather incriminating." He gestured to Dodo who revealed the bloody towel.

The inspector quirked a brow. "I see what you mean. You realize this is further evidence against your sister?"

He held the towel up by its edge for inspection, then searched in his drawer for a paper evidence bag and slipped the towel into it.

With wide eyes that watched the towel's disappearance intently, Rupert said, "I do. Lady Dorothea encouraged me to bring this to you for testing. As you may imagine I was reluctant, but when she pointed out that you would have found it if you searched my home and that would be worse for Beatrice, I came around to her way of thinking. I am confident that it is not the blood of the victim and am bringing it to you for confirmation."

The inspector placed the steepled fingers to his pitted nose. "What did your sister say when asked about it?"

"She is still in a state of some…fugue and withdrawal anxiety. We decided to find out just what we are dealing with before addressing it with her."

The inspector stroked his weak chin. "I have half a mind to march right round and bring her in again."

Rupert placed a palm on the desk.

"But I know it took a lot for you to bring this in," said the inspector. "And I appreciate your honesty. We'll get it tested and let you know what our findings are. But you must understand, if we find it to be the victim's blood my hands will be tied."

And so will Beatrice's.

Dodo decided this was the change in mood she had been waiting for. "May we ask if you have found any witnesses to the murder?"

The inspector pointed at her. "Ah yes, Lady Dorothea. I have done my homework on you. I know about your talent for snooping."

"I prefer to call it sleuthing, Inspector." She flashed her winsome smile and watched the man thaw a little. "And you must know that I have an impressive success rate."

The inspector's lower lip jutted out. "I did hear that, yes."

"Then you know I am not a mere meddler. I am an asset, and I promise to share any information I discover with you and hope that you will return the favor."

"Wait! You are already snooping around?" His fist hit the desk reminding her of a passionate clergyman pounding the pulpit on Sundays. "That is mighty dangerous, Lady Dorothea. This is not a country house where the suspects are polite gentry. This is the underbelly of the city. These are dangerous people who have no qualms about knocking off those who get in their business. I suggest that you desist immediately and leave it to the professionals."

Dodo responded with a vague answer that neither agreed nor disagreed with the officer. "Duly noted, Inspector, now to my question, have you any witnesses to the murder?"

"This is Chinatown," he said picking up a paperweight of Buckingham Palace. "No one is saying a word. Were there witnesses? Maybe. But no one is talking."

"How frustrating," said Dodo, hoping that by sympathizing she would endear herself to the inspector.

"It's just the way things are round here. Little trust in the police. But we'll get to the bottom of it, don't you worry."

"It seems such an unlikely place for Miss Stanhope to be. I met her you know, the day she was murdered in fact. She is a buyer for Livery's and I was meeting her on business."

By the look on the inspector's face, Dodo had shattered several of his pre-conceptions.

"Is that so?"

"She was a very capable woman in her field, and this is certainly not her usual stomping grounds. I have wondered why she was here in the first place."

The inspector drew a finger across his upper lip. "In my experience people have…secrets, Lady Dorothea. You can satisfy any vice you have here in Limehouse. Sneak in under cover of darkness, satisfy your needs and creep out again, no one any the wiser." He flicked the edges of the papers to his right. "Wrong place, wrong time and, bam!" He hit the desk again jolting Dodo from her seat. "You never leave."

Dodo adjusted her gloves. "Am I right in thinking your working theory is that this was a random mugging gone awry? A simple case of backstreet violence?"

The inspector's eyes slid to Rupert. "I cannot ignore a bloody knife and now a bloody towel. I must follow procedure. But if those prove to be false leads then my natural conclusion would be that this is a random act of violence, one all too often played out in this part of town."

Rupert leaned forward. "Are you saying you don't believe Beatrice is the killer?"

The inspector held up both hands. "I am not saying anything definitive, Mr. Danforth. It is too early in the investigation and there are too many unanswered questions."

Dodo watched as Rupert's stiff shoulders relaxed.

"What I can say is that we are pursuing several avenues of inquiry."

Standard line.

"Have you learned anything new about Miss Stanhope? Some of her secrets perhaps?" prodded Dodo.

The inspector narrowed his gaze. "She was a professional, single lady with no pets and no house plants. Her home was sterile and orderly. It gave us very little insight into the lady. However, the luxury of her home is a puzzle."

"What do you mean?" asked Rupert, grasping at any and all straws.

"I mean that the lady had money. Lots of it. She lived in a smart home in a fashionable area. Not something a buyer at Livery's could afford."

Interesting. I'll have to sniff around.

"And she appeared to have no friends or family. Lived for the job I'd say. Sad really. No one to miss her."

Dodo felt a stab of sympathy for the frosty woman. "Did you search her office?"

"We did." He chuckled. "Her office was as unlike her home as you could get. What a mess! Fabrics everywhere. But my officers did not find anything of interest."

The perfect place to hide something.

"And am I right in understanding that you received a tip about the knife?" Dodo asked.

"Yes, but it's of no use. I questioned the officer that answered the telephone, and the voice was muffled as though the caller had placed a handkerchief over the mouthpiece. All he could tell me was that it was an English man."

"And what about the knife? Were there any fingerprints on it?"

"A few but they were smudged too badly to do us any good." The inspector glanced at the time. "I'd better get home for dinner, or my wife will blow a gasket!"

"Thank you, Inspector. You have been most candid with us, and I appreciate it." She stood and clasped her clutch bag to her. "You'll let us know as soon as you have a result on the towel?"

"I will if you give me a number to call."

Rupert gave his number and they made for the office door.

"Now remember what I said, Lady Dorothea. No investigating round here. It is too dangerous for the likes of you." His face was stern, the geniality of the moment before, vanished.

Dodo merely smiled.

Chapter 13

"Let me get this straight," said Lizzie, horror etched on her usually friendly features. "You want me to pretend to be a customer in an opium den in Limehouse and see if I can find out if anyone saw someone plant the knife by Miss Beatrice?"

"Exactly!" declared Dodo.

Dodo had confessed that their mission had failed but had shared only select parts of their alarming experience. To do otherwise would have been to sabotage the project from the beginning.

"No!" cried Lizzie. "I've been brought up as a God-fearing girl and I have my reputation to think about. I do have my limits m'lady, and you have just hit them. I have loitered, ambushed, and who knows what else for you but this—this is too much. No!"

Dodo's heart sunk. There was no one else who could do it.

"The inspector over in Limehouse will likely be forced to arrest Beatrice unless we give him a reason not to," said Rupert gently. "I will accompany you to the door and wait outside. You just need to go in and talk to the girls who work there and see if they know anything, then say you have changed your mind. You wouldn't be in there for more than ten minutes."

Lizzie fixed a glare on him that wavered as he smiled. Lizzie sighed. Dodo knew her well enough to know that she was beginning to consider their request. She felt a hint of guilt at planning to wear Lizzie down but swatted it away. Beatrice's life was at stake.

"Would sending you to the tailor for a new dress for Christmas help at all?" Dodo asked.

Lizzie snapped her eyes over to Dodo who could see the cogs turning. They had reached the bargaining stage and Lizzie was becoming a shrewd negotiator.

"Would that dress come with a hat?"

Dodo puckered her lips. "It could."

"What about shoes?" A glint in Lizzie's eyes proved that animosity had been replaced by astute brokering.

"Certainly."

"And a mink stole?"

Dodo choked.

"Just kidding," said Lizzie slapping her thigh. "Just wanted to see how far you would go." She narrowed her eyes. "What about my reputation?"

"Do you remember when I was still at school and Daddy's horse was poisoned and we went to see a shady bookie?"

"How could I forget?" Lizzie declared.

"If you recall, we went in disguise to protect our identities. We could do the same again. I'm sure Mummy has things at the hidey hole that will work for you." She glanced at the clock. "But we would have to leave now to get ready."

Lizzie was clearly torn. Fancy dresses were her Achille's heel. Dodo waited and glowered at Rupert to warn him not to say a word. They were sitting on a house of cards and one wrong word could send the whole thing toppling. As she watched her maid decide, a multitude of expressions passed over her pretty features.

"And you would be there?" Lizzie asked, directing the question to Rupert.

"You better believe it."

Dodo hated the idea of not being where the action was, and her mind was working overtime to find a way to participate. "What if we all go?"

Rupert frowned. "Someone needs to stay with Bea."

"What if we, or rather you, ask Mrs. Prescott next door to stay with Beatrice?"

"Mrs. Prescott!" declared Rupert. "It's almost ten o' clock!"

"Exploit her crush," said Dodo with a grin. "I bet she'll jump at the chance."

The doubts that had shadowed Lizzie's face moments before, now clouded Rupert's.

She waited.

"It would be good to have you there," he agreed. "And I cannot come up with a better solution than Mrs. Prescott." He puffed air out of his mouth catching the stray curl that often fell across his forehead. "If I can face the German's, I can certainly face Mrs. Prescott. Let's get a move on before I change my mind."

"That reminds me," said Lizzie. "I stepped outside under the pretense of flicking a duster, while you were gone, and sure enough Mrs. Prescott soon came to her door under the semblance of letting out her cat. I asked her about Tuesday afternoon, and she mentioned seeing Mr. Danforth leave, and then Miss Beatrice leaving the house a little after two."

Rupert's face blazed with hope, and he grabbed Lizzie by the shoulders, planting a kiss on her cheek. Lizzie could not have looked more shocked had the queen stopped by for tea, and Dodo thought Lizzie might die on the spot.

"You wonderful, wonderful girl!" he cried. "That is fabulous news! Now we have a witness who saw Bea at the house Tuesday. No need to question the baker now."

"I don't suppose she noticed what Bea was wearing?" asked Dodo. A stoned girl would hardly have the wherewithal to change out of bloody clothes if she had committed the murder.

"As a matter of fact, she did because she criticized the fact that Miss Beatrice didn't button up her coat against the cold and that she was wearing the same clothes as the day before."

"This is very important, Lizzie," remarked Dodo. "It means that Beatrice's clothes were not covered in blood."

The clock struck the hour striking a blow at the root of the celebratory mood. "We'd better get this show on the road," said Rupert, the smile fading, replaced by an expression that might best be described as that of a patient going to the dentist for an extraction.

Dodo and Lizzie followed him to the front door and leaving it ajar, shamelessly eavesdropped.

He lifted the shiny silver knocker that reflected the streetlights and tapped gently. Within five seconds the door cracked open.

"Mr. Danforth!"

Dodo pushed the door a little more and could see that tonight, Mrs. Prescott was dressed in lilac silk pajamas with a matching bandeau holding back her graying curls. She could feel Lizzie's head above hers.

"Do you want to come in?" Mrs. Prescott said with a giggle.

Dodo watched Rupert shiver and smile through clenched teeth. "How kind of you but, no. I am aware of how late it is, but I find myself in need of some help."

The older woman leaned toward him. "Yes?"

"My sister, Beatrice, is unwell, and I need to leave on…urgent business. I am hoping you could sit with her until I get back."

Mrs. Prescott's face dimmed with confusion and unmet expectations. "Your sister? Is that the pale young woman with heavy eyes?"

"Yes, remember I told you she was staying with me."

"I do. The maid asked me if I had seen her leave on Tuesday." Mrs. Prescott pursed her lips in thought. "Why can't your maid stay with her? And when did you get a maid? She doesn't seem quite up to the task if you ask me."

Lizzie let out a grunt and slapped her hand over her mouth.

"She's on loan from a friend while my sister is convalescing, but she has to help her mistress this evening."

Mrs. Prescott's lips thinned. "When will you be back?"

"I'm not sure. Perhaps in two hours. Perhaps in four." As she wavered, Dodo witnessed the smile appear on Rupert's face that made her own knees go weak. It turned the tide in their favor.

"Oh, alright." Mrs. Prescott wagged her bejeweled finger. "But you will owe me, Rupert dear." The use of his Christian name indicated that she felt this favor had moved their relationship onto more intimate terms. "Give me a minute to settle the cat and I'll be right over." She closed the door slowly, trying for a seductive smile. Rupert shivered again as he thanked her and popped back through his own door.

"You had better beat it," he said. "If she comes and sees two ladies in competition for my attention, she will call my bluff."

Dodo put a finger on his chest. "Can you assure me she is not going to present any competition."

"I will not dignify that question with an answer," declared Rupert. "Now go!"

Dodo and Lizzie grabbed their coats and slipped to the end of the mews to wait for him.

Crammed into the back of a taxi with Rupert and Dodo, Lizzie was almost unrecognizable. She wore a pair of enormous glasses that Dodo had found in the back of a desk drawer that made her doe eyes look twice as large and a cloche hat that came down so low it almost touched the frame of the glasses, completely hiding her honey-colored curls. She sat, rigid with nerves, clutching a large, snap closure handbag on her knees.

"Why do I ever agree to these crazy ideas of yours?" she muttered, pulling a decades old, Victorian coat more tightly around her.

"Because you are a marvelous human being," said Rupert.

It was too dark to see the blush creep onto Lizzie's cheeks, but Dodo knew it was there.

"*And* you can't resist a fancy dress," Dodo added. "We will be right outside," she reassured her maid as she felt her trembling beside her.

They were all three disguised, but Rupert and Dodo were simply dressed in dark clothes to blend into the shadows.

"Remember, thicken up your accent," Dodo reminded her. "This is not one of the dens that the rich and famous frequent. This is a place for the lower classes. Do you remember what to say when you walk in?"

"I approach the girls in red and say that I need help." Lizzie's voice was wobbly and Dodo felt a pang of empathy.

"Quite. You will not need to say more to get the ball rolling, I'd wager."

Lizzie shifted her feet in the old Victorian boots. "Then I chatter on about the murder and mention that I heard they found the knife on a customer right in their establishment."

"Correct," said Dodo. "Their English may be better than they let on but speak clearly and slowly."

Lizzie made sure her hair was all tucked up in the hat. "Then I ask if they saw anyone come in while Beatrice was...indisposed."

"If they give you any valuable information from this line of conversation, you can say you've changed your mind and scarper."

"What if they don't say anything?"

"Then you might have to keep them talking by pretending to imbibe," whispered Dodo though the privacy glass that divided them from the taxi driver was closed.

Lizzie's hands flew up in distress. "I haven't the faintest idea what to do with any of it."

"Perhaps tell them you are a first timer, and they will show you," suggested Rupert.

Lizzie stiffened. "I'm not getting my mouth near that stuff! Not even for you."

"I know," said Dodo putting a calming hand on Lizzie's arm. "It will lend more credibility to you changing your mind if they know you are a newcomer."

"If you aren't out in ten minutes, I'll come in to rescue you," declared Rupert, which was very noble of him considering that they had already met Ah Lin's bodyguards. "I know the lay of the land. I can be in to get you out in a shot."

"That makes me feel a lot better," said Lizzie for Rupert's sake, but from her even tone Dodo could tell her heart wasn't in it. "This dress better be worth it!" she muttered.

"Don't forget the shoes," added Dodo.

"And the hat," said Lizzie.

The taxi slowed and Rupert pulled back the privacy glass.

"'Ere we are," said the driver. "Any place specific?"

Dodo and Lizzie peered out the window into the dark, foreboding slums. "I think I'm going to be sick," Lizzie moaned.

"Just pull up a little farther, if you please," said Rupert.

The driver pulled up to the curb and they all toppled out. Lizzie's eyes were large behind the dark frames, darting to and fro at the drunks crumpled against walls and the heavily made-up women who beckoned from the alleys.

"Ooooh. I don't think I can do this," she wailed.

Rupert slipped his arm through hers. "Of course you can. You've come this far. I will be forever in your debt, Lizzie." Her name on his lips sounded magical.

Lizzie pushed the glasses up her nose and Dodo took her other arm as they steered her toward the den they had visited earlier that evening. A small red light flickering in the window was the only indication that opium was for sale.

As they approached, a shriveled man in a grimy overcoat pushed open the door. "Let's wait for them to situate him before you go in."

"Oooh, I could do with a shot of brandy right about now," Lizzie wailed.

Rupert drew something from his pocket. It was a little silver flask. "I thought this might come in handy," he said, offering it to Lizzie. She grabbed it and took a swipe.

"I can't see a blooming thing through these glasses," she said, adjusting them as a happy drunk rolled by singing tunelessly.

"It's probably just as well," Dodo assured her. "I think it's time."

Lizzie gulped and walked like an old lady, with hesitant steps, looking back over her shoulder one last time.

A pit of remorse opened in Dodo's stomach.

Rupert looked at his watch. "She entered at ten minutes past one. If she is not out by twenty minutes past, I'm going in."

They were both hugging the wall of an alley, watching the dregs of society slope by. Blind drunk soldiers, arms round each other, singing at the top of their voices, staggered in front of them. Haggard women of the night, aged by their nefarious profession stared at Rupert as they passed. Dodo felt as though the sins surrounding them were seeping through her black coat.

Rupert slipped a comforting arm around her.

"Perhaps we asked too much of her," Dodo whispered. "What if Ah Lin suspects she is a spy and—"

"It's too late to worry about that at this point," he interrupted. "I don't imagine Ah Lin bothers with the day to day running of the place."

"Let's hope so!"

Someone began to approach them, and Rupert buried his face in Dodo's neck to avoid detection and send them on their way. Normally, such intimacy would send flutters of excitement through her, but tonight she was much too nervous to appreciate it. She turned her head in time to see the person detour away from them. Something about their gait seemed familiar.

"They've gone," she whispered.

Clouds covered the half-moon driving the shadows further into the streets and a rat ran squeaking past her feet. She would be more than ready to leave this place. Perhaps she should have heeded the inspector's advice.

"Five minutes," said Rupert, checking his watch in the moonlight.

Dodo imagined Lizzie passing into the back of the den where the stained mattresses lay awaiting their next victim.

An ill-matched couple rolled by, shrieking with laughter that sent chills of revulsion up Dodo's spine. She jumped as a piece of newspaper wrapped around her ankles in the cold wind.

Just as Rupert was declaring that ten minutes had passed, the door to the opium den crashed open and a dark figure ran screaming from the place like a bat out of a cave. It took Dodo a moment to realize it was Lizzie. She and Rupert ran after her as two black lumps were silhouetted against the dim light from the door.

What on earth happened? She will never forgive me!

"Lizzie!" Dodo cried after the fleeing figure.

Lizzie kept running until she ran straight into a red pillar box that stopped her short and sent the ugly spectacles crashing to the floor. She turned in terror as Dodo caught up and bundled her in a comforting hug.

Rupert stood behind them checking they were not followed.

"What happened?" demanded Dodo.

Lizzie could not put two sensible words together and Dodo was tempted to slap her into lucidity but refrained.

"Here," said Rupert, thrusting the flask at her. "Now, let's get out of here!"

Rupert ran into the street that was empty of cars and people. Old pages of newspapers rolled along the tarmac like tumble weeds in the Old West. Rupert turned left and right, spinning.

"We should start walking," he said.

Lizzie's eyes were half mad with fear and adrenalin and she drank hungrily from the flask. Dodo dragged her along in search of a taxi. Finally, on the outskirts of the district a lonely taxicab trundled toward them.

Rupert hailed the cab but it gave no signs of stopping. He leapt in front of it, hands up as if in surrender.

"I don't stop here after midnight," said the cabby in a crackly, cockney.

"Well, I'm asking you to make an exception," gasped Rupert, pushing the girls into the back.

Upon hearing the upper class accent the cabbie took a second look at his passengers. "What the blazes are the likes of you doing here at this time of night?"

"Never you mind," said Dodo.

"Just take us back to Kensington," said Rupert. He closed the glass between them and turned his attention to the disturbed maid.

"Tell us what happened?" said Dodo.

"He tried to kidnap me!" squeaked Lizzie.

Chapter 14

Dodo gripped Lizzie's hands. "Kidnap you?"

"The short Chinese man with the long plait, grabbed me and threatened to take me down to the cellar but years of fighting with my brothers kicked in and I slammed him hard in the shin with the boots and beat a hasty retreat." She held out a hand that was trembling uncontrollably. Dodo grabbed it with both of hers.

"I'm so sorry. If I'd known…"

"I've done some rum things for you m'lady but that one takes the biscuit!"

Dodo felt a knot of shame and guilt twist her stomach. She had been naïve not to consider the possibilities of the plot going this far sideways.

They sat in silence for some blocks, until the brandy hit Lizzie's bloodstream.

"That was too close," she murmured with a hiccup.

"Do you feel ready to tell us everything that happened?" asked Dodo.

Lizzie nodded. "Everything was going just as we planned," she began. "I slipped in and saw one of the girls in red and said I needed help. She took me back into that disgusting room, just like you said she would. Filthy mattresses and unconscious people were everywhere. Clouds of smoke made me cough up a storm and feel a little dizzy. I almost felt sorry for the poor souls." She took a breath and another drag from the flask. "Made my skin crawl to be honest, the thought of actually touching one of the mattresses. I said I was new and a bit nervous and the girl smiled at me and snapped her fingers for another girl to bring the bits." Lizzie pulled off the hat as if she were hot and rubbed her eyes. "Those glasses gave me a right headache."

Dodo glanced out the window and was happy to see that they had left the slums of the docks.

"Anyway," continued Lizzie, wiping her nose with her sleeve, something she would never have done without the brandy. "As the girl was coming over, I chattered on like I was nervous—

which I was, but not for the reason they thought— and mentioned about Miss Beatrice and all that, 'cept I didn't mention her name of course, and said I didn't want to be put on the bed that had the bloody knife. The girls smiled and led me to another." She pushed the tangled hair back from her brow and stopped her recitation as she searched for a handkerchief to fan herself. "Then I blurted out that it seemed odd that a nice girl would get caught up in a stabbing and perhaps someone had planted the knife while she was indisposed, and one of the girl's eyes got wide, and she said in broken English that she *had* seen a man come in and stand by Miss Beatrice's bed for just a moment while she was…well you know."

Rupert jumped up in his seat. "Lizzie! You've done it again! That is fantastic news. We just need to question that girl and get a description for the police."

Lizzie's gentle face took on a hardness and she set her mouth in a straight line. "Beggin' your pardon, sshir, but I am *never* going back to that place!" Dodo bit back a smile at the slur in Lizzie's words.

"Of course not," soothed Dodo. "We wouldn't think of asking you. We'll take care of it."

Lizzie's eyes found a home at the top of their orbits. Dodo had never seen her so cross.

"What happened then?" Dodo was determined to get the whole story out of her before the brandy put her to sleep.

"The second girl started laying out the whatsits and doodles and I started jumping from foot to foot and moaning that I was having second thoughts, but the first girl had gone to tell the Chinese man that I was talking about the knife I suppose, and he appears and starts yelling at me in Chinese and English and grabs me by the wrist. I was in full on panic by this time and gave him a swift kick in the shins, like I said, and took off, but not before his cronies crashed into the room and chased me. It gives me the willies just thinking about it." She started to shake again and big tears welled up in her eyes.

Dodo put a protective arm around her. "You are simply amazing, Lizzie. So brave."

"I shall buy you a dress too," declared Rupert. "Haven't seen nerves of steel like that since I was in France during the war. I would give you a medal if I could."

The hard shell Lizzie had created to protect herself from the trauma began to crack and her eyes cut over to Rupert. "Really?" she whimpered.

"Absolutely!" said Rupert. "We would never have learned this without your valiant effort. If we can find this man, it will take the attention off Bea for sure."

Lizzie settled her shoulders, drunken tears streaming down her face.

Dodo decided to summarize. "So, according to the girl from the den, Rupert's sister was already intoxicated with the opium when a man came in and stood by her bed for a moment—long enough to plant the knife and leave."

"Ah Lin is clearly not going to report this to the police—the less police sniffing around his establishment the better," remarked Rupert.

"Exactly!" agreed Dodo. "I would go so far as to suggest that it is the same man who tipped off the police."

"We really need to get a description of him," Rupert said.

"I think it's time you and I dressed in disguise and try to find the girl," Dodo said, addressing Rupert. She turned to Lizzie who was beginning to droop. "Can you describe the girl?"

Lizzie frowned. "They look enough alike to be sisters. I didn't really notice any differences."

Dodo's mouth twisted. "Then we'll just have to take our chances. I think I will recognize the girl I saw."

"But how will you know which one talked to me and which one was the snitch?" asked Lizzie. "I'm not going back there for a hundred dresses."

Dodo patted her hand. "I wouldn't dream of asking you."

"I should think not," Lizzie muttered, her head dropping onto Dodo's shoulder.

It was close to three in the morning when Dodo and Lizzie returned to the hidey hole and crashed into bed, exhausted.

By the time Dodo awoke, the sun was high in the sky. She padded out of bed and poked her head out the door to see if she could hear movement from Lizzie. Nothing.

She opened the door of her mother's Queen Anne wardrobe with its detailed wood inlays. Lady Guinevere Dorchester was a beautiful woman, but her tastes dated back a few years. Dodo pulled out an Edwardian day dress that smelled strongly of moth balls and a broad brimmed hat. If she used a scarf to veil her face it would be a perfect disguise. She hoped Rupert would be able to find something equally old-fashioned.

As she held it up to her body in front of the long, gilded mirror, Lizzie pushed in with tea and toast.

"You're going to wear that?" said the maid with a cheeky grin and smudges under her eyes.

She seemed to have recovered from the trauma of her undercover escapade. The only hint of any after-effects from the brandy were the fine lines around Lizzie's eyes.

"Yes," replied Dodo. "I need to talk to the girl at the opium den without being recognized."

Lizzie pursed her lips as she poured the tea from the pot, filling the room with the comforting aroma. "What about your voice? We all know you do a terrible cockney accent."

It was true. Dodo had attempted an accent when she was a girl and it had been a disaster.

"I'll just pretend to be French," she said in a burst of inspiration.

Lizzie lifted the silver tea strainer from the cup and laid it on the tray. "That might work."

"After we eat and I call the police station, let's go and buy you a hat," Dodo said. There was no point going back to Limehouse in the day and drawing unnecessary attention to themselves.

"Oooh! Really?"

"Yes. It's no more than you deserve."

Thinking she could kill two birds with one stone, Dodo took Lizzie to Livery's. She wanted to ask Billy more questions about Stella now that she knew about her fancy house.

As they breezed into the store, she asked the doorman for the millinery department.

"Second floor."

"This way," she chirped to Lizzie, speeding across the marble floor to the lift. As they approached the scissor gate, the lift was descending. As the contraption settled into its space and the door opened, she was thrilled to see Billy Blake smiling at the exiting customer, in his dapper uniform.

When he recognized Dodo, his face lit up with a charming smile. Then his pale blue eyes swung to Lizzie.

"And who is this vision?"

Lizzie's pretty face erupted like the red buttons on Billy's uniform. Dodo drew her gaze back to Billy with new eyes. He was a handsome boy-next-door kind of man, with even features and twinkling eyes. Lizzie was clearly smitten. The two were about the same age and their stations in life were not too far apart.

"This is Lizzie Perkins," she answered.

Billy bowed low and Lizzie's face deepened a shade further.

"I...uh...I..." Lizzie giggled.

Dodo had never before seen her turn to utter mush under the gaze of a man. The closest she had come was when Rupert had opened a door for her in Devon while they were staying at Blackwood Manor.

"You are certainly a sight for sore eyes," Billy said, his tone sincere and friendly. "Billy Blake at your service."

Lizzie put up her gloved hand and twirled a lock of hair with her finger. Dodo had to stop herself from laughing.

"Hello, Billy," Dodo said. "We are here to buy Miss Perkins a hat."

"Second floor. Millinery." He gestured with his hand for them to enter the cage. Lizzie could not stop smiling.

Since their ride was short Dodo got straight to the point. "Terrible about Miss Stanhope."

Billy's bright smile faded. "Awful. She may not have been my favorite person, but no one deserves to die like that. Alone and in a strange place."

"Yes. It's very odd that she should be in Limehouse of all places." She hoped her tone was offhand, disinterested.

The lift continued its slow journey up.

"Well, between you and me, m'lady…" He looked over his shoulder as if they were in a crowd, then whispered. "Miss Stanhope did have a little problem with opium."

Dodo pulled her gloves up. "I thought perhaps she did. Remember when I was here on Monday, and I had to go back for my umbrella? She was decidedly odd, vacant even."

"I've seen her like that too," he said. "She would often take a little between appointments. My job was to pretend not to notice."

"Perhaps she was in Limehouse to order some more?" Dodo primped her hair.

"Could be. It has a reputation as the center for things such as that, m'lady."

The lift shuddered to a stop and Billy slid back the brass scissor gate. "Second floor, millinery and notions."

Lizzie, who had not said a word since they entered the lift, dragged her eyes from Billy's face and followed Dodo out like a lamb.

"I'll see you on the way down," said Billy with a wink at Lizzie.

Dodo heard a sigh behind her. "Thank you."

The door slid closed, and Dodo confronted her maid. "Well, well. I'm surprised that you would stoop so low as to encourage the attentions of a lift attendant." She lifted a brow.

Lizzie's head reared back. "Did you see him? He's gorgeous. He could be an actor. As a lady's maid I am quite far above him in station…but I would make an exception for a face like that. Besides, he might be ambitious."

Up until now Lizzie had been a look-but-don't-touch kind of girl. It was interesting to see this side of her, a side that was probably a surprise to herself.

Lizzie was staring at the gate to the lift.

"Shall we?" asked Dodo.

"Shall we what? Oh! The hat. Yes."

Livery's was a veritable Aladdin's cave for hats and Lizzie was overwhelmed with choices and still a little distracted by the encounter with Billy. She eventually chose a plum-colored, felt cloche with a subtle band and feather. Dodo approved.

As they walked back to the lift, the apples of Lizzie's cheeks grew so tight Dodo thought they might burst. She was pretty sure the smiles were not in regards to the hat. As the lift stopped, Lizzie's hand went to her chest.

"Hello again, ladies," trilled Billy, eyes locked on Lizzie. Dodo quickly checked that Lizzie wasn't going to collapse in a puddle. She stepped on and Lizzie followed.

"I trust Livery's had what you needed."

When Lizzie said nothing, Dodo replied, "Yes, thank you. We are very happy with our purchase."

"Rarely fails people, this place."

"Indeed." Dodo checked her watch. "Who will replace Miss Stanhope? I ask only because I had business with her and will now need to conduct it with the new person."

"Her assistant, Miss Belmont, has replaced her temporarily." Billy pressed the button for the ground floor.

"Belmont? I shall be sure to contact her soon," said Dodo.

The lift settled onto the ground floor and Billy opened the gate. Lizzie was rooted to the spot.

"I should be very happy to assist you with all your needs in the future," said Billy touching his cap. "Especially you, Miss Perkins."

Lizzie pursed her lips trying to rein in a smile that threatened to get out of control. "I would like that very much, Mr. Blake."

"Oh, please call me Billy, miss. I would consider it an honor."

Dodo and Lizzie traveled to Kensington later that day to rendezvous with Rupert. Dodo raised her hand to knock when Mrs. Prescott came out with her cat.

"Oh, it's you again." She analyzed Dodo as if she were a Dover sole that was past its prime. Today, she wore a peach chiffon frock with a turban. Few women could pull one off and she was not one of them.

"I was over at Rupert's until the early hours," she announced with more than a hint of innuendo. The woman was like the burs that stuck to one's stockings after a hike.

"Is that so?" asked Dodo without the least interest, staring at the doorknocker.

"That must have sounded dreadfully inappropriate." Mrs. Prescott chuckled. "I wouldn't like anyone to get the wrong idea. Rupert is always a perfect gentleman. He had to leave on urgent business and needed my help with his ailing sister. He was so grateful when he returned this morning. I was sound asleep on the sofa, and he offered to carry me." She burst into a peal of girlish laughter. "Can you believe it?"

Dodo could not.

Mrs. Prescott had clearly not achieved the reaction she had hoped for. "What are you two up to?"

Though Dodo was severely irritated by the silly woman, there was no point causing the neighbor any ire and she had actually proven to be a valuable witness. "We're just friends of Miss Beatrice and here to visit."

Mrs. Prescott glanced at the carpet bag containing Dodo's disguise. "Staying over?"

Dodo followed her gaze. "No. Just bringing supplies." She hurried to knock on the door to cut the inquisition short. Rupert opened it and leaned forward to kiss her cheek, but she shook her head imperceptibly and seeing his neighbor, he stepped back.

"Come in."

Once they were safely inside Dodo let out a gasp of frustration. "Mrs. Prescott is a very persistent admirer."

"You have no idea," said Rupert, rolling his eyes.

"Can't she see she's old enough to be your mother?" asked Lizzie with disdain.

"She is living in a state of denial," explained Rupert.

"It may surprise you to know there is a whole army of older widows who prey on younger men, Lizzie," explained Dodo. "It has become quite acceptable these days."

Lizzie shuddered. "There are some things about the upper classes I will never understand."

They moved through to the sitting room where Beatrice was reclining on one of the couches.

"Hello," said Dodo. "Do you remember me?"

There was a sheen of sweat and a strain around her eyes that betrayed her inner struggle. "Of course. Rupert talks about you all the time."

Dodo sat on the end of the sofa. "Has your brother filled you in?"

She smiled up at Rupert. "A little. My mind is very fuzzy."

Dodo turned to her carpet bag and pulled out the antiquated dress. "Found this among Mummy's clothes. I will pair it with an outmoded hat and veil and, voila!" She faced Rupert. "What have you got?"

He put a finger in the air. "Hold on a moment." He left the room and returned with a long dark coat, narrow trousers and a light waistcoat. "Found this in a cupboard. Must have belonged to my uncle. Matches your outfit quite well."

"Not bad. Do you think you can scrounge up a monocle?"

"I believe I can. I found one when I was searching for a paper knife not two weeks ago."

"Perfect."

"Will you need me to get in some food?" asked Lizzie.

"I ordered a basket from Fortnum and Mason's for dinner," said Rupert. "Will that suit?"

"Splendid," said Dodo.

While they waited, Dodo told Rupert and Beatrice all about their shopping expedition, including Lizzie's flirtation with Billy.

Lizzie put a hand to her cheek. "I would say the flirting was all on his side, m'lady. I was too tongue-tied."

Lizzie endured some gentle ribbing from Rupert but took it with good grace.

"I would love to have a look around Stella's office," said Dodo. "I can't help feeling there might be clues that the police missed. Clues as to what took her to Limehouse that night."

A knock on the door brought the meal. Lizzie was included in the party and even Beatrice was encouraged to eat a little, though she insisted she was not hungry.

"I think getting to Limehouse after dark is a good idea," said Dodo, munching a tongue sandwich made with bread lighter than air. "I want to talk to those girls *outside* the opium den." She popped a green olive into her mouth. "We might have to wait a long time, Rupert. Are you prepared for that?"

Rupert's eyes sparkled. "More than ready! If Lizzie hadn't had that nasty experience, I'd find this all rather exciting, but her brush with danger has suitably tempered my mood and reminded me that this is not a game." He looked over at his sister with tender eyes. "But we must prove that Bea is innocent."

The huddled, weak girl unfolded a little, much as a flower bud under the first rays of summer sun. The bond between the two was evident.

Dodo finished everything on her plate and picked up the crumbs with her fingers. "I'm going to change in your bathroom. Is that alright?"

"Spiffing! I'll pop up to my room and do the same."

Dodo emerged completely veiled with the dark scarf. Her own grandmother would not know her, except that she might recognize the aged dress. When she returned to the sitting room, Beatrice jumped with fright.

"You look like a black widow," she gasped.

Dodo secured the long veil over her shoulder. "As long as I don't look like myself."

"Definitely not, m'lady," Lizzie assured her.

At that moment Rupert appeared, monocle and all. Dodo burst out laughing. Even Beatrice managed a chuckle. Rupert was having trouble squeezing his eye around the glass monocle to stop it falling out. It changed his appearance totally.

"Don't know how they wore these dashed things," he complained as the glass fell down and hung from its gold chain. A hat pulled low completed the transformation.

"Only your height will give you away," Dodo remarked. "You are much taller than the average Englishman, you know."

"It's from Mummy," said Beatrice. "She is very tall for a woman. Daddy is rather average."

"I shall slouch," Rupert said through a grin as he struggled with the monocle again.

The humor drained from the room as Lizzie warned, "Be careful. Don't forget they are very dangerous people."

Chapter 15

Even though this was now Dodo's third trip to Limehouse, she was still surprised by the meanness of the streets. It was hard to believe that this was in the same city as Buckingham Palace, Westminster, and her own family's luxurious hidey-hole. Litter was strewn everywhere, and the saddest types of souls continually roamed the streets.

And the smell.

It was a dock town, and the Thames was not the cleanest of waterways but the smell of fish heads and guts, mingled with the drains for the sewers, made it almost unbearable tonight.

She and Rupert had the bemused taxi driver drop them off on the periphery of the neighborhood, keeping to the shadows, and then crept around the back of Ah Lin's opium den in search of a back alley. They were now stationed by a dilapidated fence watching the den's back door.

Something bumped Dodo's shoe. She screeched and looking down, saw a mouse scurry away. She shuddered.

"Don't like mice, eh?" Rupert asked with a chuckle.

"Not particularly but, if you must know, snakes are my biggest fear."

"Not too much danger of those in England. The three types we have are pretty harmless."

"Oh, it's not the venom that frightens me," she explained. "It's something about the way they move and how they look. Fear grabs me like a cat dropped in water, and my legs turn to jelly."

"Then I know how to surprise you," he joked.

She elbowed him in the ribs. "I'm warning you now—don't try it!"

He put his lips close to her ear so that she could feel the vibration of the sound. "Are you threatening me, Lady Dorothea?"

"You'd better believe it!" She adjusted the veil. "What scares you, Mr. Danforth?"

He didn't hesitate. "War."

Dodo half-turned to him. "Oh, of course. How very insensitive of me. I was just trying to fill time. Please forgive me."

Putting both hands on her shoulders he said, "I didn't mean to make you uncomfortable, Dodo. It's just anything else that scares me pales in comparison. But as a boy I was scared of the dark and frogs."

"Frogs?"

"Yes, some of the chaps put one in my bed at school when I was eight and frightened me to death."

"Poor little you." She ran a finger down his cheek.

"Did *you* go to boarding school, Dodo?"

"I was a day girl. The first time I left home was 1920 when I went to finishing school in France at seventeen."

"So, you speak French?"

She chuckled. "I do, but my French friends cringe at my pronunciation. I say the words as though I am speaking English apparently, and they prefer talking to me in English."

"My accent is pretty awful too," said Rupert. "The farmers would scratch their heads when I was trying to explain about the horses. I never became fluent."

"I can read—"

The door at the back of the establishment opened and two men she had not seen before walked out into the alley and cut to the left. Dodo and Rupert pushed themselves up tight against the fence and her dress caught on a protruding nail.

"I didn't recognize them," said Dodo after they had safely gone.

"Me neither."

She unhooked her dress. "Have *you* ever taken laudanum or the stronger opium?"

"A doctor gave it to me once when I broke my leg falling off a bally roof, and I had some pretty nasty side effects. Itched from head to toe, and it did something odd to my vision for a while. That was enough to make me steer clear. You?"

"Not really. I think someone gave it to me as a child and it made me excessively sleepy and disoriented. I didn't like the feeling. That's the same reason I don't drink much."

"All sorts of things were offered to me in the army, as you can imagine, but I could see what it did to the fellows out there and they couldn't leave the stuff alone when they got home. I've never been tempted. It kills me that Bea is in its clutches and—"

The door scratched open again and Dodo saw a flash of red. She moved out of the shadows as the figure stepped into the moonlight and recognized her as the girl she had met at the reception desk. There was a fifty-fifty chance she was the one who had spoken to Lizzie.

Dodo dropped to the floor as if searching for something.

"You cannot be here," said the girl in a heavy Chinese accent, moving toward Dodo.

"I dropped an earring," said Dodo with a French accent. "My 'usband and I are trying to find it." Rupert slid into the light coming from the open door.

"I don't care. You get in big trouble if boss man finds you." The girl looked behind her to the door.

"Are you scared of 'im?" asked Dodo, straightening.

The girl nodded, her beautiful dark eyes hooded with fear.

"Why are you so frightened?" Her throat was starting to complain as she forced the accent.

The girl tipped her head in the direction of the den. "He mad. Nosy lady. Now he angry at everyone."

This was just the type of opening Dodo had hoped for. "What was zee woman being nosy about?"

Experience told her that when people are indirectly involved in an infamous crime their pride is flattered and they cannot help but mention it.

The girl moved closer. "You hear 'bout murder?"

Dodo nodded and Rupert joined the group.

"Young lady come in ask questions. Mr. Bossman, he crazy that killer plant knife here. Get him in trouble with police." Her long, straight hair shone in the light of the moon.

"Zat is terrible," said Dodo. "Did you say someone planted zee knife 'ere?"

"Yes. I saw the man, but I stay quiet."

Dodo pulled off her veil and the girls eyes widened with recognition.

"You!"

"Please help us. This man's sister is being accused of the crime. Can you describe the fellow? If I can find him, I will be able to tell the police that your boss is not involved."

The girl clasped her hands and looked back at the door.

"I know him."

"He was someone you know?"

"Yes. That's why I no tell boss. I like him. He good to me."

"What is his name?"

The girl turned to go, and Dodo reached out and caught her wrist gently. "Please. We are desperate."

"I don't know his real name. I know him as *Pigeon*."

The girl was walking back to the door. Dodo's chance was slipping away. "What does he look like?"

"Young. I must go."

"Is his hair dark or light? Does he speak like the people here?" asked Dodo.

"Dark. Nice eyes. I go now." She made a shooing motion with her hands. "You go too. Dangerous."

"Thank you," whispered Rupert as the girl disappeared, swallowed into the dark building.

As Dodo and Rupert entered the police station, the chairs were lined with the usual hard luck cases, and a couple of drunks were serenading the crowd. Tonight, the station smelled just like the docks and Dodo wrinkled her nose. The night desk sergeant was the older man with the jowls and as Dodo unwound her veil his eyes popped out of his head.

"Welcome back, m'lady," he exclaimed when he had gathered his wits about him.

"Good evening, sergeant," she said, flinging the veil around her shoulders. "I should like to speak to Inspector Wadley, if he's here."

"Right oh!" he said, disappearing through the grimy glass door.

106

Rupert took her in his arms and began dancing to the drunken singing. She couldn't help but laugh after the tension of the evening.

"Am I interrupting something?" the inspector said.

Rupert dropped her arms but kept hold of her hand.

The inspector looked them up and down. "I very much hope that I am wrong in thinking that you have been doing a little police work this evening. It's not Knightsbridge, you know. We have enough trouble keeping up with all the criminals, let alone having to rescue the likes of you getting caught between their crosshairs."

Dodo arranged her features into a look of studied umbridge and looked down at her dress. "Careful Inspector. This is one of my favorite outfits." Then she winked.

"Through here," he said, shaking his head and opening the door. "You know the way."

In his tired little office, they told him everything that had happened from Lizzie entering the den the night before to talking to the girl in the alley. From the grunts and groans emanating from the man of law, she perceived that he was not a champion of her methods.

Inspector Wadley huffed through his lank mustache. "By gum! You could have all been killed. They don't value human life round here."

Dodo waved a hand back and forth in contradiction. "But as you see we are safe and we have gathered valuable information, have we not?"

The inspector straightened his tie. "You have, I'll give you that. My officers hit a wall of silence from the people in the den. Pretended they couldn't speak English."

"You have to admire her, Inspector," said Rupert. "Lady Dorothea may be scared of snakes but not shady thugs in drug dens."

Dodo rewarded him with a bright smile. "Now, do you have information to share with *us*, Inspector?"

"As a matter of fact, I do," he said pulling out a paper from under a neat pile. "Firstly, the blood on the towel was not human."

Rupert let out a yelp of relief. "Thank heavens!"

"And secondly, after seeing Miss Stanhope's residence, we looked at her bank account. She had an unusually large amount of money. We checked to see if she had received any kind of inheritance and could find no evidence of such."

"So where did it come from?" asked Dodo, continuing the inspector's line of thought. "Are you thinking she stole the money?"

The inspector dipped his chin causing it to triple. "That is an ongoing line of investigation, so I am not at liberty to disclose our theories."

"But if she did, it might be a motive for her murder," declared Dodo. She tapped her chin. "Have you been to her home, Inspector? How lavish was it?"

"Not by your standards, Lady Dorothea, but she certainly lived in a style above her obvious means."

I wonder if Billy has any insights.

"That would not explain why she was in Limehouse, though," said Rupert.

"Well, if she had an addiction to opium, that might bring her here," said Dodo. "Just like it brought Beatrice. And if someone was following Stella and knew she had a lot of money on her..."

"So, we are back to a random mugging then," said Rupert.

The inspector's head was swinging left to right as they speculated, as if he were watching a tennis match at Wimbledon.

Rupert stopped and faced the inspector. "By the way, does what we found out let Beatrice off your hook?"

"Someone higher up the chain will have to make that call, and since I only have your word for it..."

"Ah, yes I see," said Rupert, with less energy. "But you will follow up with the girl?"

The inspector leaned back and stapled his fingers; his signature move. "I'm not sure you understand how hard it is for the police to make any inroad in this community, sir. That young girl will shrink like a tortoise into its shell and pretend not to understand a word we say if she thinks it will get her in trouble. We can ask around to see if anyone else knows him but it's not much to go on. A young man with dark hair and kind eyes whose nickname is Pigeon."

Unless Dodo could figure out who this Pigeon was and question him, it would be hard to shift the investigation away from Rupert's sister.

As things stood, Beatrice was still suspect number one.

Chapter 16

Billy opened the scissor gate and a woman, trying desperately to hold back the tides of age, stepped out. A saleswoman carrying a pile of boxes followed her.

When Billy spotted Dodo his face split into a wide grin, revealing uneven white teeth.

"Lady Dorothea," he began and then lowered his voice, his eyes darting left and right. "We must stop meeting like this." He slapped his knee, straightened his cap, and looked around her. "Miss Perkins not with you today?"

Dodo's lip curled. "Not today." She needed his full attention.

"Where can I take you? Ladies' wear?" His finger was poised by the buttons.

"Actually, I was hoping to ask you a few questions."

Billy tilted his head.

She lowered her voice. "Can I rely on your discretion?"

"Discretion is my middle name, m'lady." He tapped the side of his nose.

"It has been discovered that Miss Stanhope was a lot wealthier than one would suppose."

A line formed between Billy's eyes. "What are you saying?"

"I'm saying that she was rich and did not need to work here." Dodo studied his expression. If she had to pick one word to describe his reaction it would be incredulity. Then he broke into another smile. "Perhaps they pay her a lot better than they pay me."

"Billy, I need you to take this seriously. Can you think of any indicators that she was securing another means of income?"

Billy tipped his cap back and rested his chin on a fist. "Not that I can think of. To be honest she didn't say more than two words a day to me. She demanded efficiency with the lift and that I be ready to escort her clients down at a moment's notice. That was about it."

"Did she ever meet with people who did not seem to have anything to do with her work?"

Billy's mouth shrugged. "No. All above board, I'd say." He leaned forward. "So, what do you think? Was she stealing? Selling merchandise at a higher price than agreed and skimming off the top?"

The hunger for gossip in his eyes gave Dodo pause. "No idea. I am trying to build a picture of the woman, and this is an anomaly."

A salesgirl headed toward the lift but on seeing Dodo, made an about turn.

"Beggin' your pardon m'lady, but you work and don't need to," said Billy, settling his cap back on his head.

"That is true but my work is more of a hobby. Miss Stanhope was here working full time I gather. And she was not from a wealthy family. In fact, I believe both of her parents are deceased."

Folding his arms, Billy said, "Well then, see there, you know more than me."

A military type of gentleman approached the lift. Dodo made a decision. "Is Miss Stanhope's replacement in?"

"Miss Belmont? Yes, she came in early since the police are done with the office."

"Can you take me to her, please," she said as the other customer gestured with his arm for her to go before him. She stepped inside the cage and the tall man followed.

"Third floor," he commanded.

"Third and fourth floors," said Billy drawing back his professional mask. "Ladies first!"

As Dodo stepped out into the fourth-floor hallway she turned. Billy was saying something serious to the gentleman, but she could not hear what he was saying.

She approached Stella's door and knocked.

"Come in!" This time the voice was bright, sunny and welcoming.

A woman in her early thirties greeted Dodo, blonde waves tucked up and held with a pencil, ringlets trailing down each side of her delicate face. "Yes?"

Dodo took a seat, explaining who she was. "Miss Stanhope and I had agreed on Livery's buying a few of next season's line.

111

At the risk of seeming insensitive, I'm just checking the order will go through despite her unfortunate passing."

"Let me see," said the woman in a breathy voice. The desk was full of papers and the swatches of fabric still took up every inch of floor space. "Stella, Miss Stanhope, appears to have had a haphazard system," Miss Belmont explained, an apology in her eyes. "Each fabric swatch has labels attached which I assume is some kind of filing system—I just haven't worked it out yet."

Dodo looked around the mess. "But you were her assistant. Surely she explained it to you?"

Miss Belmont addressed her remarks to the ceiling. "I don't like to speak ill of the dead and her passing is a tragedy," she began. "But Miss Stanhope was very protective of this office. She would meet me in my small, cramped one down the hall rather than here." She leveled her gaze at Dodo. "So, I'm stuck trying to make sense out of chaos. I do apologize."

If Stella had been ice, Miss Belmont was the sun in spring.

"Oh, it's entirely my fault," said Dodo. "I should have made an appointment instead of springing myself on you. I was just in the area and thought I would check that you are still onboard for the three designs Stella chose."

"Only three designs? Did you have more?" Miss Belmont swept some curls behind her ears. "I know enough about the House of Dubois to appreciate that it is one of our most popular brands. Can you come back with the portfolio? Now that I am in charge, I'd like to take a look at the whole line."

"Of course," said Dodo, standing. "I'll make an appointment."

Miss Belmont lifted her graceful hand. "It was lovely to meet you, Lady Dorothea. I look forward to our next interview."

As Dodo went into the hallway, leaving Miss Belmont to the task of digging out from under Stella's lack of organization, she was surprised to see the lift gate open and Billy speaking to the same gentleman.

"Lady Dorothea!" he exclaimed. "You took less than fifteen minutes." He chuckled. "I thought Miss Belmont was the type who would give clients more of her time."

Dodo nodded to the other occupant who gave her a strained smile that didn't reach his eyes.

"She will, I'm sure. I had not made an appointment and she is still trying to get organized. It was my own fault."

The lift settled onto the ground floor and Dodo exited as the other gentleman strode across the marble floor to the main exit doors.

She stopped. "I'll be back soon for a scheduled meeting," she explained.

"Will Miss Perkins be with you?"

"Perhaps. Goodbye, Billy."

Beatrice was shaking and crying. Not the kind of tears one sheds after a stubbed toe or a twisted ankle, this was deep, from the marrow, anguish. It made Dodo shudder.

"I've tried to help her," said Lizzie who had moved to the door to whisper to Dodo. "She's reached the point where she needs professional help in my opinion. I did try to mention it to Mr. Danforth…"

It was time for an intervention.

She found Rupert nursing a coffee mug in the kitchen looking as though he had just learned that his favorite pig had been slaughtered.

"A penny for your thoughts," she said.

He looked up, his beautiful face etched with sorrow. "This is dreadful. Lizzie has been marvelous, but I think…"

"…it's time to tell your parents." Dodo said the words that were so hard for him.

He deflated right in front of her. "Yes. But I am dreading it."

"Didn't you say Veronica needed to dry out somewhere?" Veronica was the horrid woman who had persecuted Dodo at school and had a similar problem to Beatrice. Rupert had become entangled in a scheme with her because she had helped Beatrice out of some bother before. "Where did they take her? Do you know?"

His haunted blue eyes slid to the right. "Why didn't I think of that? It was a place in Surrey…" He snapped his fingers. "Downsmeade Convalescent Home."

113

A glimmer of hope sprang from his face. "I could take her there, get her settled and *then* call my parents. Do they need to know about the arrest and everything, do you think?"

Dodo slid her arms around his neck and leaned her cheek against the top of his soft hair. "One bridge at a time, my darling. This alone will be a shock to them. I think you wait until your hand is forced—which it might never be if I can solve this case. And it seems that our investigations have provided enough doubt as to Beatrice's guilt that the police have not released her name to the press. Wait a bit until it becomes unavoidable. That's what I would do."

"I shall make arrangements immediately. The poor girl is suffering so." He jumped up in the direction of the telephone.

Dodo went back to the sitting room. Beatrice was worse, rocking back and forth in absolute misery.

"Please tell me you persuaded him," said Lizzie, whose own eyes were frantic.

"He didn't need much persuading, actually. He's making the arrangements now."

The door burst open. "They have a place available and can take her today."

"How will you get there?" Driving in a taxi all the way to Surrey would cost a fortune but taking Beatrice on the train would expose her to public derision.

"I shall use my car."

Dodo's eyes bulged. "You have a car?" She had no idea as they had always used taxis and trains.

"A sweet little roadster. Utterly impractical but a beauty. Just enough room for the two of us and a place to strap a suitcase on the back."

"Where on earth do you keep it?" Dodo asked.

"There are old stables at the end of the mews, and I store it there."

"Show me where the suitcase is, and I'll pack a bag for Miss Beatrice," said Lizzie.

The two of them rushed up the stairs and Dodo went to the telephone to call the inspector and inform him that Beatrice would be in a nursing home. But she had another motive; to try to sweet talk Stella's address out of him.

It took no time to pack, and Lizzie and Dodo helped Beatrice into a coat and hat that shielded her face.

A roar outside took Dodo to the door. Sitting out front was a small, black and green, Chevrolet, A Series roadster in tip top condition. The noise inevitably brought out Mrs. Prescott. She looked Dodo up and down with distaste.

"Going for a ride?" she asked Rupert, as her cat's diamond collar glinted in the weak winter sun.

"Yes, taking my sister for a ride in the country," said Rupert with false enthusiasm.

"Isn't it rather cold? Is she feeling better?" Mrs. Prescott had on a thick, cream woolen dress and a lilac cashmere shawl.

"Nonsense! I'll put the hood up and blast the heater and nothing could be better."

Lizzie shuffled Beatrice out the door and settled her into the only other seat, pulling her hat down to avoid Mrs. Prescott's prying eyes. Rupert hurried to strap the suitcase to the back.

"So, you're staying over?" she asked Dodo.

Really! Dodo's limit had been reached with the nosy neighbor, even if she was helpful at times.

Dodo ignored the impertinent question.

"Ta ta!" she said, encouraging Rupert to leave forthwith as he opened the driver's door and slid in. She wanted nothing more in the world than to grab him by the collar and kiss him till his knees buckled but the current circumstances made that impossible.

Waving, he thundered to the end of the street as the three women waved back.

"There is something seriously wrong with that young lady," said Honoria Prescott as she stood watching the empty space where the car had last been.

"Nothing that a bit of country air can't cure," said Dodo as she pushed Lizzie back through the door and slammed it shut.

Chapter 17

The inspector was right. The street where Stella had lived was very fashionable, just inside Chelsea. The chic townhouses were made of white stone with pretty wrought iron balustrades, shiny black front doors, and large brass handles.

Much too nice for a buyer at Livery's.

Each house had its own steps leading up to the front door, a fan window over the top, and a railing leading down to a basement, where in days gone by the kitchens would be bustling with scullery maids and cooks. The whole street screamed prosperity and status.

As Dodo stood at the top of the street she smiled, remembering Inspector Anderson's voice as he begged her not to bring shame on the police department by any unseemly antics.

As if!

Since permitting her entry to Stella's home was completely against police rules, Dodo had decided to question the neighbors. Her plans were loose so that she could be inspired in the moment. Now, seeing the respectability of the street she was sure she could get herself invited into tea at least twice.

Stella's door was just like the others with a brass number eleven standing out from the black gloss paint of the door. No other decorations or ornamentation encumbered the entrance. It was neat and without fuss—just like the owner.

The door to the left was similar but boasted a shiny, blue pot containing decidedly dead plants, and a cat with its back to the pot staring at Dodo with penetrating green eyes. She strode up the four steps and lifted the brass lion's head knocker and then turned her back to the door to survey the quiet street.

As the door behind her opened, she twirled around to behold an elderly maid in her black and white uniform, a feather duster in her hand. The maid quickly placed the duster behind her back.

"Can I help you?"

Dodo handed her a card. "My name is Lady Dorothea Dorchester, and I was acquainted with the woman who lived next door. Miss Stanhope. I am devastated by her death and was hoping to meet some of the people who knew her. Do you think your mistress could give me a few moments of her time?

The honorific title was like a key to the city.

The maid allowed Dodo to enter and bid her wait while she presented the card to her employer.

The entry hall was quite narrow, but the fan window let in enough light to make it seem wider. The floor was black and white marble, with a rich nineteenth century, mahogany vitrine cabinet providing relief. The cat had let itself in and was washing its paws by the foot of the stairs. Dodo was admiring its delicate movements when the maid returned with a secret smile.

"The mistress will see you now."

She led Dodo to a door just off the entrance hall and ushered her in.

"My darling girl!" yelled a white-haired lady, sitting in a high back chair, hands in the air.

"Mimi!" cried Dodo and rushed to embrace her grandmother's old and revered friend, Lady Madeline Parker. "What on earth are you doing here?"

The happy chance of finding Mimi during her investigation was like a sign from the universe that she was on the right track.

"After Arthur died and Alan moved into the big house, I decided I wanted to live in town and be amidst all the action. I love the ballet, the opera, the museums, and can visit whenever I please." Her eyes sparkled with excitement. "Now, how is the Dowager?"

Mimi Parker had been friends with Dodo's grandmother since childhood. She was known for always carrying black licorice in her pocket.

"Granny is in fine health. She comes to dinner with us at least once a week but rarely ventures as far as London anymore."

"The last time I saw her was near the end of the war, I think. Not long after your grandfather died. She writes, of course. A fine old girl. One of my dearest friends."

The maid returned with a glittering silver tray laden with a pot and rosebud china, and fresh, dainty cakes. Dodo's mouth watered.

"Thank you, Ellis," Mimi said and set about pouring the tea. Handing Dodo a cup she asked, "Now what is all this nonsense about Stella?"

Dodo narrowed her eyes. "Has Granny ever told you about my...hobby?"

"The fashion thing? Yes, I think it's absolutely marvelous!" Mimi clasped her arthritic, wrinkled hands under her chin, a man's ring winking at Dodo from her fore finger.

"Actually, I was talking about my other hobby—sleuthing?"

Mimi frowned as though she had misheard.

Dodo tried again. "I have a knack for solving crimes. Granny didn't mention it?"

"Ah, I am not familiar with the word, sleuth. Yes, the Dowager did write something about it. Isn't it rather macabre?" She was peering out at Dodo from under thinning white eyebrows.

"It can be, but it is so satisfying to obtain justice for the person who has been killed."

"If you say so, dear." Mimi took a bite of a tiny, fairy cake with butter cream icing.

"Well, that's what brought me here today," explained Dodo.

Understanding blossomed across Mimi's face. "Poor Miss Stanhope," she said, nodding. "Did you *really* know her?"

Dodo placed her cup and saucer on a small table. "As a matter of fact, I did. I had met her the morning of her death as it happens. I'm sure you know she was a buyer for Livery's, and I had an appointment to show her the new spring line from the fashion house I represent. I was so shocked to hear that she had been murdered." Dodo shifted forward in the deliciously comfortable armchair. "But my connection to her gets even more strange." She explained about Beatrice.

Mimi put her cup on the occasional table and placed both hands on her knees giving Dodo her undivided attention. "That gives me goosepimples! It's like some kind of hex."

Dodo shrugged. "So, you see, I simply must investigate."

Mimi raised a brow.

"And I think I am in love with her brother, Rupert."

118

The frown transformed to a knowing smile. It was the first time Dodo had admitted it out loud, other than to Lizzie, and it felt…right.

"Tell me all about him, dear," said the woman whose days of romance were long behind her.

Dodo was happy to oblige and told Mimi all about how she and Rupert had met, how her first impression of him had been awful and how he had won her over. "So here I am," said Dodo, after finishing her tale. "Desperate to vindicate his sister." She took a long sip of the comforting brew. "I was hoping to get some background on Stella by getting myself invited to tea by someone on the street. Running into you has been like winning the jackpot." She took a breath. "So, what can you tell me about Stella?"

Mimi squinted as she considered the question. "She was not the friendliest neighbor. It is customary to visit neighbors when one moves in and take tea, but Stella moved in two years ago and never did. Snubbed us all, in fact. That did not sit well with the street, I can tell you." Her milky eyes moved left. "I saw her on the step once or twice and I said 'hello' but she barely responded. I could tell she was not from our set. Didn't have the necessary manners." The cat jumped onto Mimi's lap and she absentmindedly stroked the silk, black fur. "I think she gutted the place when she moved in—all kinds of decorators in and out. I shudder to think what she did to the place." The room they were sitting in was distinctly traditional, dripping with velvet and lace.

Dodo felt her hopes of discovering something useful, fade. "So, you have never been inside?"

"No, like I said, she did not obey the social rules of high society. Kept completely to herself."

"You are absolutely right, she is not from old money," said Dodo. "I also happen to know that she did not receive a significant inheritance of any kind upon her parent's deaths, she is not of the aristocracy, and she works at Livery's. So here is my question. How on earth did she afford such a place as this?"

Mimi started tapping the cat's head so that the animal winced and closed its elegant eyes. "As you know, I am not nosy by nature, but I do love to sit in this front room, and I sometimes see things."

Dodo's pulse kicked up a notch. "Go on."

"She had gentlemen callers." Mimi took a long sip, staring at Dodo.

This was not what Dodo had expected. Stella was such a cold, hard person. "Really?"

"Same few. A younger man, an older, upright man, and a foreigner."

"A foreigner?"

"A Chinese man in traditional garb."

Dodo's blood ran cold. "Did he happen to have a long plait that hung down his back?"

"Yes, how did you know? He chanced to turn my way as I was watching one day, and I saw it. Not stooped at all…"

Dodo had stopped listening. Stella knew the man who had tried to abduct Lizzie!

Finally, here was the answer to why Stella was in Limehouse so late on that fateful night. Dodo's brain started churning and drawing conclusions. She was going to see Ah Lin.

Didn't Mimi mention a younger man?

Mimi was still talking but Dodo interrupted. "You said there was a younger man?"

"He only came on rare occasion and wore a hat down over his face so I could not tell you what he looked like. But I could tell he was younger than the other gentlemen from his gait and stance."

The girl who worked in the opium den had said the person who planted the knife on Beatrice was a young man whom she knew. The pieces were starting to come together.

"The older gentleman helped me into a taxi one day," continued Mimi. "Lovely manners, he spoke with the diction of a colonel. Made sure I was situated before he left."

An image of the man in the lift jumped into Dodo's mind. "Was his hair reddish with a matching mustache?"

"Yes. Have you met him?"

"I think so. I know the Chinese man too which is far too many coincidences." Dodo smacked her knee causing the cat to jump

120

off Mimi's lap. "We have a single woman, working for a living, owning a home in a neighborhood she should not be able to afford and receiving visits from the owner of a sleezy Limehouse opium den."

She locked eyes with Mimi. "I believe Stella was dealing drugs."

Chapter 18

Dodo, Lizzie and Rupert were back at the hidey hole in Mayfair away from Mrs. Prescott's prying eyes. Beatrice was safely installed in the convalescent home and Rupert had alerted his parents with a dose of understatement.

Lizzie had bought one of every pastry available at the bakery round the corner and they were enjoying high tea for lunch in style, eclairs, chocolate bombs, tarts, and bread pudding.

The sun had barely made it out today, providing no defense against the chill, and a friendly fire danced in the grate. If it wasn't for Beatrice's addiction and the murder, all would be right with the world.

The murder.

Dodo told them all about finding Mimi and what a trove of information she was.

"I remember her," said Lizzie. "She was the one who brought licorice and would treat all the maids with a piece."

Rupert reached for his third pastry. "Our unsavory gentleman from the den was a regular visitor at Stella's? It is so hard to believe."

Lizzie shuddered and folded her arms across her chest. "If I never see him again it will be too soon."

"I have concluded that the only reason she would meet with someone like Ah Lin in Limehouse is to conduct business. She must have gone there to meet him, and for some reason he killed her. It is the simplest explanation."

Lizzie yelped. "He would have killed me too, I reckon."

"If he proves to be Stella's killer, then you are right, Lizzie. I'm sorry I ever put you through that. Can you forgive me?"

"You weren't to know he was a murderer, m'lady."

"Thank you," said Dodo, wrapping an arm around Lizzie's shoulders.

"Should we tell Inspector Wadley what you have discovered?" asked Rupert. "A witness who has seen Ah Lin at Stella's home, the knife being found at his establishment and the drug connection. It's more than enough to bring him in for questioning."

"We could," she said, watching the flames flicker. "Perhaps we should. But I just don't feel settled yet. How do the red-headed chap, and the fellow the girl called Pigeon, fit in? And what about the young man Mimi saw? How do we know one of them didn't kill Stella? And why would Ah Lin plant the knife in his own place? No, I feel like we are still missing an important piece."

She rested her head on Rupert's shoulder. "I need to find out more about Stella, and her double life and how she intersects with all those other people."

"What about her assistant, Barbara Belmont? Aren't you supposed to meet with her? You could use the occasion to ask questions."

"Golly! I forgot about that." She glanced at the carriage clock on the mantle. "I'll call right now."

"Well, hello Miss Perkins," said Billy, beaming from ear to ear. "I've counted the days since we last met."

Lizzie's cheeks burned bright as the noon day sun in summer under the new hat she had purchased just a few days earlier. "Go on with you!" she chided.

Billy put his hand to his chest. "I promise you, Miss Perkins. You have been a shining light in my week. Beauty like yours is a rare thing."

Lizzie did not know where to look but was grinning from ear to ear. She shook her head. "What a load of codswallop!"

Billy pantomimed disappointment. "Lady Dorothea, can't you assure her that I am in earnest?"

"Lizzie, I do believe Billy is being sincere, though I am not sure you can totally trust him after so short an acquaintance." She wagged her finger at him.

All joking slipped from his face, and he placed his right hand over his heart. "I assure you that I am trustworthy," he said, facing Lizzie. "I'd be honored to take you out to tea or for a walk along the river some time."

Lizzie's beautiful, round, blue eyes opened wide. "I'd like that," she murmured.

"You would?" He punched the air with a triumphant fist. "You just made me a very happy man, Miss Perkins."

Dodo cleared her throat.

"A thousand apologies, m'lady. Which floor?" His eyes dropped to the portfolio. "Fourth?"

"Yes," said Dodo. "I have an appointment with Barbara."

The lift lumbered its way up and she and Lizzie stepped out into the hallway.

"Thank you, Billy. I don't know how long I will be."

Billy winked. "At least with Miss Stanhope I knew when to come back."

"Miss Belmont must be a better person to work for, though?"

"Oh yes. Loads better. Much less persnickety."

Dodo knocked on the door and Barbara's friendly voice called them to come in.

Dodo gasped.

The office was unrecognizable. Gone were the mountainous swatches of fabrics, revealing colorful rugs and tasteful furniture. "I love what you've done with the place," she said with a chuckle after introducing Lizzie.

"Thanks! It took me forever," said Barbara who was now sitting quite relaxed on the other side of the clean desk. "But I just couldn't work with that kind of clutter and mayhem."

"I suppose some people thrive in chaos," said Dodo.

"Not me," declared Barbara, pulling on her classic blue blazer. "But I must confess that as I was gathering all the swatches to put in that little ante-room" —she pointed to her left—"it was obvious that Stella did have some kind of system. Each swatch had two tags containing numbers and letters. One matched the numbers in the account books, but the other didn't. I couldn't figure it out so I just had to start all over again. I was here till three in the morning two nights in a row."

Dodo could see that Barbara had tried to use make-up to hide the smudges under her eyes. She pulled out her portfolio. "You probably knew Stella better than anyone. She doesn't seem to have had family or close friends, according to the newspapers."

Barbara extracted the pencil from her hair which fell to her shoulders in blonde ringlets making her look much younger. "That may well be. I've worked with her for three years now and she never mentioned any family or friends to me."

"What was she like to work for?"

Barbara moved a hole punch that didn't need moving. "I learned a lot, but she was...difficult. She would change her mind all the time."

"What do you mean?" asked Dodo, sliding the leather portfolio case next to her chair.

"She would call me for a meeting—always in my cramped office—and give me a hundred things to do. I would starve myself trying to get them all done before our next meeting and then she would forget she had asked me to do anything. I would bring it up and she would wave the notion away and give me a whole new list. It was hard to keep up." She leaned across the desk. "I had to go to the doctor for ulcers caused by stress."

"Strange," said Dodo. "Stella appeared so cool and collected—except for the messy room."

Barbara lowered her voice. "She was like Jekyll and Hyde." Dodo remembered her own, similar conclusion. "Before she, uh, died," continued Barbara, "I was thinking of asking for a transfer. I just couldn't take it anymore."

"Well, you seem to have restored everything to its proper order. Are you up to the task?"

"I am more than ready," she said clasping her hands. "Except for the promotion coming at the expense of Stella's life, it is a dream come true." She reached her open palm across the desk and Dodo proffered her the portfolio.

"So, you are Stella's official replacement?" asked Dodo. "Billy seemed to think it was a temporary position."

"Yes," replied Barbara. "It was made official yesterday morning."

"Congratulations! I shall look forward to working with you."

"Thank you!"

The new fashion buyer for Livery's examined each sketch carefully. "These are outstanding," she cried leafing through the sheaves of paper. "Magnificent! I believe these will fly off the shelves." She looked up fixing Dodo with a confident stare. "I am interested in all of them."

"Splendid! I can see that you appreciate couture. Frankly, I was surprised when Stella only liked three of the designs." Dodo picked up her gloves. "I'll let Renée know. She'll have everything ready by spring."

"May I keep the sketches for a while? They will give me inspiration for our advertising and window campaign."

"Of course."

"Is there anything else?" asked Barbara.

"I *was* hoping to look through the swatches. When I was here before I was yearning to touch them, but I was afraid to ask Stella and she dismissed me so quickly. I think I could recommend certain of your fabrics to Renée." This was a half-truth. Stella's comment about the two tags on the swatches had piqued her interest.

"Certainly." Barbara stood. "Follow me, Lady Dorothea."

Lizzie had sat wide-eyed during the whole interview. Dodo imagined that she was still thinking about Billy's offer. She tapped her on the shoulder.

They accompanied Barbara to the anteroom. The fabrics that had been scattered around Stella's office were now in neat piles that almost reached to the low ceiling.

"I'll leave you to it," said Barbara. "I'm going to the accounting department to adjust the budget for the purchase."

Livery was famous for its bold and floral fabrics and the stack did not disappoint. Dodo pulled a particularly bold design from the middle of the pile and turned it over. There was the label Barbara had referred to pinned into the corner. Another label was sewn into the finished edge. She studied the attached one and saw that it held the codes for what she assumed to be dye colors, the designer of the pattern, and the weight and length of the fabric.

What is this other one for?

She studied it. There were initials and several groups of numbers.

126

"What do you think this is?" she asked Lizzie.

"It looks like those labels from the cleaners." Lizzie pointed to the letters. "This would indicate whose laundry it is and these," she pointed to the numbers, "look like dates and times." She handed it back and Dodo looked again.

Lizzie was right.

"You are so clever," she said.

Lizzie's head reared back. "For knowing about laundry?"

"This is the kind of thing I know nothing about. Priceless information. Can you copy these down?"

They spent the next fifteen minutes noting as many labels as they could before Barbara returned and they said their goodbyes.

Billy was just opening the lift gate when they left Barbara's office.

"Miss Perkins, have you thought any more about my proposition? My heart is waiting."

The usually chatty Lizzie was unable to say a word.

"How about the day after tomorrow? It's my half day," he suggested.

Lizzie's mouth gaped open and shut like Lord Alfred's koi fish.

"That should be fine," Dodo said, as voice for her mute maid. "Should she meet you here?"

"Nah, let's meet at the park near the Lyon's tea house. I get off at two. We can meet at a quarter past."

Before Billy could close the gate a tall man in a salesclerk's uniform rushed in.

"Good afternoon, Mr. Turner," said Billy.

"Good afternoon. Fourth floor, please."

"I have to take these two fine young ladies to the ground floor first then I'll go back up."

"Perfect," said the clerk through discolored teeth.

They rode down in silence and Billy let them exit, repeating the time and day for the date. He then turned to the man who remained, referring to him as Jack.

Dodo took several steps forward then grabbed Lizzie's arm.

"Jack Turner. Initials J.T. What date is it? December 5. That's the numbers 12 and 5." She checked her watch. "And it is just on two o' clock."

Lizzie gasped. "J.T. 5.12.2! It's a filing system. But for what?"

"Opium," said Dodo.

Chapter 19

Dodo was pacing back and forth over the plush Persian rug, reciting the facts as they knew them thus far. As usual, listing things out loud helped her brain sift and filter, making things clearer.

"If every swatch of fabric that has the extra tab represented an opium customer, I think we are alleging that Stella was the head of a large, drug ring." She stared at Lizzie and Rupert waiting for their verdict on her summation and conclusion.

Rupert was digesting all the information by rearranging all the magazines on the coffee table. "It would certainly explain the expensive house and meeting with Ah Lin. The other two men who went to Stella's house must be part of the ring too."

"Yes, because I saw one of them at Livery's on one of my visits," Dodo said.

"I can't believe it!" declared Lizzie. "A respectable lady like that. And in such an important department store. Boggles the mind."

"Drugs make people do things they normally wouldn't," said Rupert. "What begins as something you try at a party or to relax after a stressful day at work, soon gets out of hand as evidenced by my sister. And it is an expensive habit. What better way to fund your own addiction than to sell to others? Stella clearly had a knack for business, or she wouldn't have the position she did at the store. From small beginnings it just grew."

"Aren't we also saying that many of her clients are staff at Livery's?" said Dodo, running her finger round the top of her teacup.

"Which means that Stella was running a shadow network of drug distribution alongside the legitimate business of the department store?" said Rupert.

"Blimey!" said Lizzie.

"It's a great cover. Who would ever suspect Livery's of nefarious dealings?" said Dodo considering the extent of the operation.

For a moment, the room was quiet, only the noise of traffic and pedestrians outside breaking the silence. Rupert smacked his forehead, pinning Dodo with his bottomless blue eyes. "We are assuming that it is secret. What if it's not? What if Stella was a lower player and upper management is involved?"

"Crikey!" gasped Lizzie

"I'd say we have got to a point where this is much too big for the three of us. It's probably time to update Inspector Wadley and let him take it from here," said Rupert.

"Hold on a minute, my brain is still grinding away," said Dodo. "Let's leave the conspiracy theory and get back to Stella's murder and why she would have been in Limehouse if the other players did their business with her at the store or at her house. Why go into the lion's den, so to speak?"

The mantle was decorated with various souvenirs from all over the world and she picked up a silver bell from Italy. "Let's assume for our current purposes that Stella's murder was not a random act of violence but that she was targeted," said Dodo, taking the bell and sitting in her mother's favorite armchair, kneading the silver ornament and causing a little clinking noise. "What reasons might a top tier drug dealer have to leave their own territory?"

"Dissension? Perhaps she had to go in person to sort something out, like distribution," suggested Rupert.

"Distribution. Yes! Perhaps Ah Lin was jacking up the price and she wanted to confront him."

"They could have argued, and he or his bodyguards could have killed her, like we suggested before," said Rupert.

"Yes!" said Lizzie.

"No!" said Dodo at the same time.

"Explain," said Rupert to Dodo.

"Stella was killed in the street outside Ah Lin's own den. Why would he leave her body outside his business and bring the police sniffing around? He could have had his goons dispose of the body quickly, so no one was any the wiser. The river is right there." She placed the bell on the table. "And if he had murdered her, he would certainly not have planted the knife on someone in his own den. He would try to throw suspicion on someone else or throw it in the river too. Then Stella would just be another missing person."

Lizzie's puzzled face mutated to agreement. "I have to concede. Your points make a lot of sense, m'lady. Only an idiot would implicate themselves."

Dodo took a deep breath. "I think all those things rule Ah Lin out, as the murderer at least."

"That brings up another point," said Rupert. "If it was not Ah Lin who killed her, why was she killed out in the open, right in front of *his* den and not in a back alley?"

"Excellent observation!" Dodo put both hands to her face, breathing deeply through her fingers. "Why in such an obvious place?" She started waving her hands excitedly and pointed at Rupert. "Because someone was sending him a message. A warning. Cross me and this will happen to you."

"Perhaps one of the other players was giving themselves a promotion?" suggested Rupert, and Dodo took a moment to appreciate how adorable he was when energized by a new idea.

"Genius!" she said, grabbing his hands, wanting desperately to kiss him but fighting the urge so that she did not embarrass Lizzie. "Let's start with the other three men we know of. The man I will call the 'colonel', that helped Mimi into the taxi, the young man who came to see Stella at home, and the fellow the Chinese girl knows, the one she saw plant the knife."

"Did she mention if he was Chinese too?" asked Rupert.

Dodo snapped her head. "Drat! She didn't. I assumed he was not, but she didn't say. She said he was young, dark haired and kind. There is no way she is going to talk to me again."

"He could be the murderer, or he could work for the murderer," said Rupert.

"Well, we can't do much about him right now. But I can try to find out the identities of the other two men who called at Stella's house, and worry about him later." She stood. "I should go back and talk to Mimi."

"Would you like me to call the inspector about the drug ring at Livery's?" said Rupert.

"Thanks for the offer but I think I'll do it. The more I vocalize the plot the clearer it becomes. I'll go and call him right now then head to Mimi's."

She put through the call and threw all the conclusions they had drawn and the unanswered questions, at the inspector. After fifteen minutes she returned.

"Well, the poor chap is reeling. Feels that it is outside his pay grade and is calling Scotland Yard to go and question the management at Livery's. I hope it doesn't make the lower levels of this thing scatter like cockroaches. Perhaps I should pop back to talk to Billy now before it all blows up. He seems to have his ear to the ground and maybe he can tell me about the 'colonel'. Do you want to come?" This last was directed at Lizzie whose cheeks splattered with color at the suggestion.

"Uh, no thank you. We're supposed to go out for our date tomorrow. I'll wait till then."

"As you wish." She glanced at her watch. "I can get there by four if I leave now."

"Do you want me to come?" asked Rupert.

"No, I think that will make Billy clam up. He knows me and I am sure he is a fount of gossip. I need to tap into that. I'll go to Mimi's right after so have tea without me, but I'll be famished by dinner time."

"I'll make a reservation at Pierre's, shall I?" asked Rupert.

"French? How open minded of you." Dodo looked at Lizzie who dipped her eyes. "I'll be fine. There are some eggs I can whip up for myself."

"That's settled then. See you later."

It was a cold, wet December afternoon but Dodo was feeling warm under her fur collar as she hurried past the doorman of Livery's and toward the elevator.

Billy's eyes lit up as she approached. "Lady Dorothea, how lovely to see you again. Another appointment with Miss Belmont?"

"No," she began. "As a matter of fact, I have come to talk to you."

A middle-aged woman approached, and Dodo stepped aside. "Lingerie," she said to Billy who motioned with his head to indicate that Dodo should step inside.

"Third floor," Billy announced, and the compartment went quiet as the box lumbered up the shaft. Dodo stared at her shoes that had suffered at the hands of the dirt and rain outside.

"Lingerie," announced Billy as he opened the gate to the lift and the woman stepped out. Dodo had not been to this floor and looked out with interest. As she did so, a salesgirl who was walking toward the elevator saw her. The girl's eyes slid over to Billy, and she did an about turn, reminding Dodo of one of her other visits when a young male salesclerk had done a similar thing. Perhaps there were rules about staff using the elevator when a customer was occupying it.

A light lit up indicating that someone on the ground floor was waiting for the lift. Dodo seized her chance.

"Billy, I have been intrigued with the death of Miss Stanhope."

"As have we all," said Billy pulling the gate across. "Terrible."

"I mean. I have been looking into it."

Billy pressed the button for the ground floor. "Is that so?"

"I dabble in detective work," she explained.

Billy turned, surprise on his face. "A society lady like you?"

The lift rocked as it started its descent.

"I find it very satisfying work," she explained, an eye on the lights of the panel. "I have discovered something rather huge, and I am wondering if it's general knowledge among the staff."

"Now I'm really intrigued," he said, adjusting his cap.

They had two floors to go. "Would it surprise you to know that Miss Stanhope was running a drug ring here at Livery's?"

Billy's jaw dropped open. "Miss Stanhope? Surely not!"

His surprise was an indicator that it might not be as widespread an operation as she had thought. "I need you to think about the types of people who were coming to her office. Were they all like me or were there salespeople, delivery people,

133

cleaning staff? You know, people from all different levels of society?"

Billy folded his arms in thought just as they settled onto the ground floor and the bell tinged. A mother and two young children were waiting outside. Dodo stepped back as they entered.

"Children's shoes," the mother said.

"Second floor," said Billy.

They rode up in silence but as soon as the mother and children exited, Billy whipped round to face Dodo. "I've been thinking about your question and the answer is no. Mostly well to do people like you or managers. She wasn't the type to give time to the lower classes."

"What about the man who was here the other day? The military type with the reddish hair and moustache. Is he a regular?"

"Oh yes, I remember him. He comes in every now and again, but he gets his shirts from here."

"He has never been to see Miss Stanhope?"

Billy grimaced. "No. Why would he? He's just a regular customer here. Why?"

It is too much of a coincidence that a man Mimi sees at Stella's door regularly and that I see here is not connected to all this.

Dodo decided to try a different tack. "Was Miss Stanhope nice to you?"

"Depends on what you mean by nice. I was well below her on the pecking order. She was sharp when letting me know what was expected but after that she left me alone." Billy kept shaking his head in disbelief.

"Is there another way up to her office?" Dodo asked.

"There's the back stairs or the front grand stairs."

"And you have no inkling of the kind of operation I am suggesting?"

Billy swiped off his cap and drew the arm across his forehead. "None. It's like something that might happen in America, but here? Nah."

134

"Well, Scotland Yard are coming to investigate the matter very soon. They will probably have questions for all the staff."

"Thanks for the tip," said Billy. "But I don't know nothin'!"

"Twice in one week! How lovely!" said Mimi as Dodo bit into a cream puff. *I shall have to watch it, or I shall be as fat as butter soon.*

"Are you here to question me again?" The black cat was on Mimi's lap staring at Dodo with suspicious eyes.

"I do have some follow up questions." Dodo dabbed her red lips with the napkin leaving a pinkish residue. "Remember how I suggested that Stella was involved in selling drugs? Well, it's a much bigger operation than I thought. As incredible as this is to believe, it appears that Miss Stanhope was the kingpin of a drug ring operating directly out of Livery's."

Mimi jerked with surprise and some of her tea spilled onto the saucer. "Good heavens!" she cried.

"I believe the men you saw visiting her were lackeys of her operation."

"Criminals right next door?" Mimi's hand went to her chest and the disturbed cat jumped off. "Oh, my goodness! I feel all at sixes and sevens."

Dodo put down her cup and came to kneel by her old friend, grasping her hand reassuringly. "I doubt that you were ever in any danger, but now that Stella is dead the threat has passed." She hoped that her words were true. She would ask Scotland Yard to post someone at the house next door until the case was resolved.

"My heart is racing," Mimi declared.

Dodo held her hand for several minutes until the old lady's blood pressure had returned to normal. "There, there. I am so sorry to have upset you."

"I consider myself quite spunky, courageous if you will, but the idea of criminal activity just on the other side of my wall, well, that's something else altogether." Mimi dabbed at her wrinkled cheeks with a lavender scented, lace handkerchief. "The shock has passed. Was there something else, dear?"

"I crossed paths with the military looking gentleman you mentioned, at Livery's on one of my visits. At the time, it meant little to me, but now that we have an idea of what his business with Stella was, I know his presence at Livery's must be significant. However, the lift operator assured me that he never took the man to Stella's office at the department store. It's a puzzle. Anyway, I'm wondering if you can remember anything else about the other man. The younger man you saw?"

Mimi's eyes blinked in concentration. "As I said, he kept his face shaded and never really turned my way."

"Perhaps you heard his voice or noticed the type of clothes he wore?"

Mimi's head snapped to a tilt. "That does make me remember something. I heard a pigeon cooing. I remember I looked out because they are dirty, messy birds and I didn't want any of its mess on my steps and I was about to call my maid to shoo it away, when I realized that the sound was coming from the young man."

Pigeon!

Dodo's heart jumped. That was the nickname the Chinese girl had mentioned. Could they be one and the same man?

"That's good, Mimi," said Dodo encouragingly. "What about his clothes?"

"Just an ordinary black coat with the kind of hat every man wears." She twisted in her chair. "Oh, I'm so sorry, Dodo, I can't remember more. I should have paid closer attention."

"Nonsense! You could have no idea it would be important."

The tea cakes lay forgotten.

"Well, I should be going," said Dodo. "I am sure they won't be back now that Stella is gone, but it goes without saying that if you see either of them again, steer clear. And give me or the police a call."

The maid let her out and she stood at the top of Mimi's steps, staring at Stella's front door.

"Who killed you, Stella?"

136

She tried to imagine the man in the dark coat and hat. She was sure he would be a source of valuable information that held the key to the crime if she could only find the mysterious man.

Chapter 20

Scotland Yard Investigates Livery of London!
The morning newspapers were full of the raid by Scotland
Yard. It had happened while Dodo was at Mimi's the evening
before; after the store had closed but before the management left
for home. Much of what the journalists had written was
guesswork— they did not really know the reason for the raid but
evidently someone had tipped off the press.

Now that she understood what the labels on the swatches
stood for, and the Yard had completed their interviews, Dodo was
itching to get back and see if there were any fabrics left in the
anteroom. However, having told Inspector Anderson of her
discovery, she presumed they had all been confiscated in the raid.
She would just have to try and match the labels they had
managed to record against a list of employees, at some point.

Barbara Belmont had said she could come back at any time, so
Dodo made another appointment. She wanted to see for herself
how rattled the staff were after the raid and if there was anyone
who did not show up for work.

Lizzie's date was scheduled for that afternoon and did not
accompany Dodo. In fact, she was in a right state. Babbling
uncontrollably, pacing the floors and constantly checking her
appearance. It occurred to Dodo that Lizzie had only experienced
romance through her and her sisters, and that it was high time she
had a little for herself. And Billy seemed harmless enough.

She waved to him from across the marble floor and he
switched on his thousand-watt smile. Lizzie was going to be
putty in his hands.

"Lady Dorothea. A pleasure to see you again." He gave her a
cheeky wink. "I'm all ready for my date with Miss Perkins. I had
a shirt cleaned special and its waiting in my locker."

"I shouldn't be telling you this, Billy, but Lizzie is a bag of
nerves. She's a complete novice at this kind of thing, so treat her
gently."

"I am nothing if not a gentleman," he replied, touching his cap.

"I have no doubt," she replied.

"Where to today?" he asked.

"I have another meeting with Miss Belmont." She took out a compact mirror to check her lipstick and give her eyes somewhere to be. "I read about the raid."

From the corner of her eye, she saw Billy's countenance drop in disbelief. "Can you imagine? A great old store with a fine reputation being raided?"

She closed the compact and slipped it into her handbag. "Were you here?"

"I was in the staff changing room, but the news spread like wildfire through the building."

"Was anyone...particularly concerned?"

Billy jerked his head round to look at her. His lips twisted. "Now you mention it, there were a couple of nervous faces. Mr. Conner in haberdashery and Miss Wainwright in lingerie. I didn't put two and two together at the time but now..."

The lift bell dinged. They had arrived at the fourth floor. "This is you, m'lady."

She wandered down the hall and cast a quick look back. Billy's expression was like none she had seen on him before. He must really love the old store.

She knocked on the door and was welcomed in by the breezy tones of Barbara.

"Lady Dorothea, how lovely to see you again. I gathered up some fabrics I thought you might like. If you will follow me?"

Dodo followed her into the anteroom that had been full of the piles of swatches. As she had feared, they were all gone.

Dash it!

"Oh dear," she began. "I had seen a swatch the other day that I particularly liked and was hoping to discuss with you."

Barbara's brow clouded. "Yes, I have no idea why, but Scotland Yard came and took the lot."

"Every single piece?" Dodo asked.

"There is one I still have that I had stuck in a drawer to use later."

139

"Could I see it? I know it's a slim chance that it is the one I liked, but you never know."

"Of course. Hold on a minute." Barbara disappeared back into her office and returned holding the square that had escaped the clutches of Scotland Yard.

"That's it!" lied Dodo, though the fabric was a dull paisley more suited to her mother's generation than a new spring line of couture.

"Really?" exclaimed Barbara holding it up to inspect. "I thought it was a bit dowdy myself."

"Not for a whole outfit but for a scarf or a hat bandeau. I think it would work marvelously."

Barbara clearly did not agree but was too polite to contradict a member of the aristocracy. She handed the swatch to Dodo but proceeded to show her the bolts she had brought up from the fabric department.

"Any idea why Scotland Yard is so interested in Livery's?" Dodo asked, all innocence as she looked through the beautiful bolts.

Everyone of Dodo's senses was energized by the bright designs, the flowing silks and chiffons, as she ran her hands over them. For a moment she forgot her mission and stepped into her role of fashion connoisseur.

"None," replied Barbara. "No one told me anything. I am completely confused, but they only seemed to be interested in the upper management. Kept them here till all hours I heard. I can't imagine. Perhaps one of them has embezzled funds?"

"Very possible," said Dodo, relishing the softness of the silks. "This and this," she said as Barbara tried to keep up with writing down the numbers. "And this, oh and this." A child in a sweet shop could not have been more satisfied. Dodo pointed out ten more and then smiled while Barbara continued scribbling the numbers down. She took the moment to look at the labels on the swatch.

B.B. 11 5 12 5 1 5 2 5

It was unlike the others with many more numbers. She couldn't seem to make sense of it.

"I shall have samples cut for you. They should be ready by tomorrow," said Barbara.

"Excellent. I shall take them to Paris on my next trip. I know Renée will adore them. Perhaps we can advertise that the fabric is exclusive to Livery's."

"That would be a great feather in my cap as I establish myself as Stella's successor." Barbara placed the lists in a manila folder.

Time to get back to why you really came.

"Can I take this swatch?" Dodo asked. "I think I will use it as inspiration."

"Since it was from Stella's time, I think that would be fine," said Barbara. "I feel that I am going to take women's fashion in a whole new direction. Bring Livery's into the twentieth century."

"Bravo!" applauded Dodo. "Make your mark, I say."

Barbara walked her through to the office and opened the door. "I see this as the beginning of a very profitable partnership, Lady Dorothea."

"I do hope so." She stepped into the hall to see Billy waiting, whistling like birdsong. "Goodbye."

"Meeting go well?" he asked.

As she stepped in, she glanced at his name tag.

Billy Blake.

B.B.

She looked up to find him staring at her with dead eyes.

Her mind started spinning. A younger man seen by Mimi, the whistle that sounded like a pigeon, his connection to Stella, the shadowy figure in Limehouse she thought looked familiar.

Billy.

Her body went rigid, and she forced a smile on her face. "Very well, thank you. I think I'm going to like Barbara a lot more than I liked Stella."

"Everyone does," said Billy, his voice flat.

She watched in horror as they glided past the ground floor and descended to the basement.

With her heart in her throat she asked, "Where are we going, Billy?"

Chapter 21

"You know." There was no inflection in his words. It was a statement.

Her mind was buzzing with possible options, which were few. "Know what?"

"You have figured something out. I can tell from the way you looked at me when you stepped in." The handsome, friendly face she was used to was gone. His jaw and eyes were hard as steel.

The words of the young woman from the opium den passed through her mind. *"He is young. Nice to me. They call him 'Pigeon'."* Probably meaning that he wasn't nice to others.

The lift rumbled to a stop and Billy caught her wrist in a vice grip. She could scream but she was quickly drawing the conclusion that Billy was Stella's killer. He would have no qualms about killing her. And who would hear her in the basement anyway?

He pinned her arm behind her back, and she felt a prick through her coat.

He had a knife.

That changed everything.

"Move it!" His tone was fierce.

She shuffled forward, searching around for another person but the dingy space was empty of people, full of boxes, machinery, and noisy pipes.

"You should have kept your nose out," he murmured. "No reason for a lady like you to get involved. Now I'm going to have to get rid of you."

She had been in tight spaces before but never really alone. Someone was always with her or coming. A cold sweat broke out all over, adrenaline flooding her veins as a wave of panic threatened to rob her of clear thought.

Don't succumb to hysteria. Breathe.

Billy pushed her toward a door and opened it to reveal a neglected, small storage room. He let go and thrust her in holding the knife aloft. Bending, he grabbed a coil of rope and started to bind her hands.

"Several people know where I am," she said, hoping her voice sounded more confident than she really was. "If I don't arrive home soon, they will start looking for me." This was not entirely true. Lizzie was heading out by now to meet Billy for the date. And she had failed to tell Rupert of her plans.

Stupid girl!

"No one will find you down here," he sneered. "And tonight, I'll make you disappear. I have a talent for it."

"I told the police I suspected you," she threw out, her voice reaching a pitch she was unused to.

Billy stopped and stared at her, then dropped his gaze and continued binding her wrists. The rope bit into her flesh. "You're lying."

"Is that a chance you can afford to take?" she said matching the steel in his eyes with her own.

"Once I've popped you, I'll disappear and reinvent myself. New name, new address, new everything. I've got lots of money stashed away."

She kicked out at him, but he caught her foot and reaching for another length of rope began to bind her ankles.

She screamed.

He slapped her across the mouth and the tang of iron filled her mouth.

"That was a stupid thing to do. I have no qualms about hurting you. I'd kill you now, but it would make a mess and I have business to take care of." He wagged a finger at her. "But I can always change my mind. Is that what you want, m'lady?"

The fire in his eyes was evidence enough that he was telling the truth.

This was the real Billy.

The friendly lift operator was the act.

When he was satisfied with his work he pushed back onto his haunches. "So, what gave me away?"

"I figured out Stella's filing system," she replied. "And your whistle. Birdsong. I'm guessing it is sometimes pigeon."

Billy's lips hitched to the side. "It's a habit I need to break."

"Why did you have to kill her?" Dodo asked.

"She treated me like dirt. Her operation would collapse without me but when I demanded a bigger share of the profits she laughed in my face. I told Ah Lin to demand a meeting at his den. I promised him that if I got a bigger cut, he could negotiate one too." He laughed and it was demonic. "Stupid twit believed me. Then he learned to fear me."

Pulling a kerchief from his pocket he gagged her.

Checking his watch, he said, "I'd better finish my shift. Don't want to raise any eyebrows, now, do I?"

She wriggled to try to free herself, but she was bound tight.

Billy's eyes narrowed. "Now you stay here, nice and quiet and I will consider killing you quickly with as little pain as possible. But if you try anything…well, let's just say I'm not the boy scout I appear to be."

He locked the door and Dodo was left in complete darkness with only the sounds of the heating system for company.

Her shoulders drooped. How could she have been so thick-headed?

She allowed herself a small moment to wallow in self-pity then tore herself off a strip.

Rather than sit and stew, put your bally brains to work.

She reviewed the things she now knew.

Billy was the young man that Mimi had seen regularly at Stella's house, and the man the Chinese girl told her about. One and the same. He was well placed at Livery's to be involved in a drug ring since he moved about the store for his job and his false persona was above suspicion. Who would consider the amicable lift operator a criminal? The red headed military man was obviously an accomplice and Billy had lied through his teeth about him when questioned. Everything he had ever told her was probably a lie.

Billy had murdered Stella.

Billy had framed Beatrice and Ah Lin.

Her eyes began to adjust to the darkness, and she could just make out rough shapes. It looked like a pipe ran across the back of the storage room. She pulled her knees up to her chest and scooted her backside forward telling herself to ignore the fact that she was ruining an expensive angora skirt. After several failed attempts she made it to the pipe. Raising both feet she banged the metal. It clanged loudly.

Dot. Dot. Dot. Dash. Dash. Dash. Dot. Dot. Dot.

She blessed her father for teaching her the basics of Morse code. She waited a few minutes then repeated the sequence. She had to find a way out of here before Billy returned. She prayed that he would not meet Lizzie for their date.

Would he hurt her?

Dodo had arrived at the store around eleven and Lizzie was supposed to meet him at a quarter past two. She tried to calculate the time now. It must be at least one o' clock. Would anyone even miss her before evening?

To keep her mind from sinking into depression she continued to work out the crime. Stella had been the leader of the operation and, unable to keep traditional records of deliveries, had created the swatch system. It was ingenious. She presumably kept her legitimate job here at Livery's to keep her above reproach.

She thought back on the different employees she had seen who had approached Billy in the lift but changed direction when they saw her. He must have been the go-between or delivery boy. So many people addicted to the terrible stuff.

But why kill Stella? Rupert's suggestion came back to her, a desire for promotion. Billy had said Stella looked down on him. He must have become greedy, seeing all the money she was making, and decided to take things into his own hands. By killing Stella and implicating Ah Lin he had made a power play—mess with me and this will happen to you. He would assume full control of the operation, wielding violence against anyone who tried to oust him.

She tapped out her message for help again and strained her ears.

Nothing.

Hours had passed and she was simply bursting to use the ladies.

Every few minutes she would tap out the Morse code but with each unheeded attempt she was less hopeful. The floor was hard and her behind was beginning to go numb. And she was angry. Angry that if nothing changed, she was going to be killed before she had really had a chance to live. And what would it do to Mummy and Daddy? And her sister, Didi? She flattered herself that they would never recover.

And Rupert.

She had finally met the man of her dreams and they would never have the chance to see where things took them. Her heart squeezed in her chest. She loved him.

Stop this! It's not helping.

Instead, she replayed their last kiss.

Had she known it would be their last, she might have played things differently, but they had not known that tomorrow would not come. As Rupert had left the flat last night, she had slipped into the hallway with him to prevent Lizzie feeling awkward. He had tugged her to him, like a cowboy might pull a girl with a lasso, holding her hips in his warm hands and whispering against her lips until she ached for him to kiss them. Tendrils of anticipation danced between them, her stomach twisting in knots until his lips met hers. The smell of his cologne—

The sound of footsteps shattered the precious images like a broken mirror, and she tensed.

Billy was back.

She pulled up her legs ready to thrust them at her opponent, but though the handle moved the door didn't open. She tried to shout but the gag muted her efforts.

A hard bang on the door burst the lock revealing two blessedly familiar silhouettes, one short, the other tall.

"Dodo!"

Rupert!

She made guttural sounds as Rupert ran to untie her and Lizzie stood with her hand to her mouth, tears streaming down her cheeks.

Rupert loosened the gag and took her in his arms, kissing her until she went limp with relief and joy.

Lizzie's hands were over her eyes.

146

"Could you untie my hands and feet now?" she asked when Rupert finally released her, hope restored and a lilt in her tone. "How on earth did you find me?"

Rupert looked at Lizzie. "You have your maid to thank for that," he said.

Lizzie. Dear, faithful Lizzie.

Not waiting around to be found by Billy who could return at any moment, they opted to flee the basement through a window. Rupert smashed the filthy glass with his elbow and helped Dodo and Lizzie through. Dodo's skirt caught on the sharp edges, ripping a hole in the soft wool as she climbed out. As Rupert lifted her off the window ledge, she scuffed the fine Italian leather of her shoe on the rough, plastered wall.

It's just 'stuff'.

Within minutes they were in a taxi on their way to Scotland Yard.

Dodo let out a huge sigh and hugged her maid. "Tell me everything."

Lizzie swallowed. "Well, I was all of a dither, waiting for Billy and everything, that I got there way too early. When he didn't come right on time, I didn't think anything of it but after fifteen minutes I started to worry that I got the day wrong. But when I looked in my diary, I knew it was the correct day." She took a breath and Dodo wanted to scream at her to hurry up, but she bit her lip instead.

"After half an hour, I decided he had stood me up which I wasn't really surprised about—"

"Balderdash!" cried Dodo. "You are *much* too good for him."

"Thank you, m'lady, but I'm no looker."

Dodo elbowed Rupert.

"What rot!" he declared on cue. "You are as lovely as a spring morning, m'dear."

This caused Lizzie to have an attack of bashfulness and Dodo waited impatiently for her to pull herself together.

"As I was saying, I wanted to give Billy the benefit of the doubt but after three-quarters of an hour I knew for sure he had stood me up." She brushed a curl back under her hat. Dodo suppressed a shriek.

"I decided to go to Livery's and see if he had been held up or something," Lizzie continued as dirty buildings and pedestrians flashed by. "I knew it was stupid and I wasn't going to approach him or anything but if he was still working then that would explain things. But when I got there and looked through the window, Billy wasn't the lift operator."

Now we are getting somewhere. Dodo's leg was bouncing up and down uncontrollably.

"I was trying to decide if I should go and talk to the new boy or cut my losses by walking around the street thinking, when I happened to look up and caught sight of Billy getting into a taxicab. It made me angry thinking that he was maybe taking someone else out, so I ran up the road to see if I could see if anyone else was in the cab." Lizzie blew her nose.

"Well?" demanded Dodo as the taxi hit a pothole and sent them all vaulting out of the bench seat. Rupert rubbed his head.

"It was the owner of the opium den, Ah Lin! I will *never* forget his face!"

"Gadzooks!" cried Dodo. "So, you immediately knew Billy was one of the bad guys."

"Yes! I did an about turn before they saw me. Then my nervous mind went into over-drive, and I began to think. I ran to a phone booth and called you m'lady but no one answered, so I rushed back to the hidey-hole and there was no note. You *always* leave me a note, so I knew you had not been home. I called Mr. Danforth to see if you were there. When he said no, I told him what I had seen."

"When Lizzie called me, I thought it odd that you hadn't telephoned about anything you had learned in your meeting," said Rupert taking up the tale. "And since we knew that Billy was involved and you were missing, my sixth sense told me something was wrong." The arm around her shoulder squeezed. "I told Lizzie to meet me at Livery's. If Billy was a player in the drug ring perhaps you had stuck your nose into the wrong place and got into trouble. When we got there, we popped into Miss Belmont's who confirmed that you had met with her and then went down and asked the doorman if he had seen you leave. 'Now that you mention it, sir' he said, 'I have *not* seen the lady leave which is strange since she came in a little before lunchtime and always says goodbye.' That made my blood run cold."

He nodded to Lizzie who had turned in her seat so that her back was against the door. "I agreed with Mr. Danforth that something was wrong and that you must have made some discovery about the murderer which had got you in a pickle. It's a bit of a habit of yours." She dug Dodo in the ribs. "We asked ourselves what would happen if Billy was also the murderer? He could hardly murder you in the middle of the store to keep his secret."

"Or take you out the main entrance or the delivery door which would be full of workers," said Rupert. The tag team delivery would have been cute at any other time, but Dodo dug her nails into her knees.

Get on with it!

"Lucy, my sister works at a store in Chadminster and they have a basement where all the workings of the building live. It's dark and dirty and you only go down there if you really have to."

For the hundredth time Dodo inwardly praised Lizzie's large industrious family.

"As soon as Lizzie told me that, we rushed down here," said Rupert. "We could hear nothing but hissing steam and clanking machines until after a few minutes I heard a more regular knocking."

"Me!" squealed Dodo, ready to wrap up the story. The adrenalin rush had morphed into an energy crash. She leaned her head on Rupert's shoulder, utterly exhausted.

"Well, I didn't know it was you at the time. I only caught the end of the sequence as it happened, so we stood still and listened again. Ages later—"

Dodo's head snapped up.

"I'll have you know that I had been banging for several hours and was hungry and tired," she protested in her defense.

Rupert's eyes smiled a tease. "*Ages* later, I heard it again, the Morse code signal for distress." He kissed her firmly on the cheek.

"Good job he was with me," added Lizzie, "because I wouldn't have had a clue."

Good job indeed.

A shiver of fear ran through her spine as she considered the fact that she could still be imprisoned, waiting for Billy to come and kill her with no one the wiser.

Chapter 22

Standing outside Scotland Yard, Dodo took a deep breath.

The last time she had been here was with Charlie Chadwick and Chief Inspector Blood when the room had filled with romantic tension—but not between her and Charlie.

She whisked the memories away. Charlie was history. If Blood was here, she would cross that bridge when it came. She had bigger things to worry about.

Still trembling from her ordeal, she took Rupert's hand and plunged through the door.

An overly cheerful policeman stood behind the reception desk, eyes bright and uniform spotless. "Can I help you?"

"I have information on the murder of Stella Stanhope and the drug operation at Livery's."

The pencil dropped from the constable's hand. "I'll call upstairs. Please take a seat."

The contrast between this waiting room and the one in Limehouse made Dodo smile. It was clean, white, and empty of people. She almost missed the drunken singing.

The door opened and her heart hiccupped, and the stress made her feel faint after all she had already been through.

But it was *not* Chief Inspector Blood.

She wasn't sure if she was relieved or disappointed. It would have been useful to measure the two men against each other to see how strong her feelings for Rupert were in the face of someone she knew set her feelings humming.

A burly, whiskered man extended a hand to Rupert. "Chief Inspector Morris. You have information for me?"

"Not I, sir. Lady Dorothea Dorchester." He motioned toward Dodo.

The man clearly recognized her name. He smiled and it was like looking at Father Christmas. "Your reputation precedes you, Lady Dorothea. It is an honor to meet you."

Dodo rewarded him with her signature smile and witnessed the usual effect. "Am I to understand that you are the officer in charge of the murder?"

"Actually, I am the head officer for the raid on Livery's. I think we have you to thank for the tip off on that one, though after interviewing the upper management we don't believe they have any involvement, other than Miss Stanhope, of course."

"That's why we are here," said Dodo. "We know who the new ringleader of the drug operation is and the identity of Stella Stanhope's murderer."

The chief inspector's face suffused with surprise. "Then come this way and let me take an official statement."

When the three of them had finished, Chief Inspector Morris leaned back in his chair. "By gum! You're lucky to be alive m'lady."

"I am well aware of the fact, Chief Inspector. Now, what are you going to do about Billy Blake?"

"He thinks you are still bound tight in the cupboard, right?"

She glanced at the clock. Darkness was falling in the capital city, but the store would not close for another hour. "He said he would deal with me after the store closed, and all the employees had left. I don't think he would return before that as it might raise suspicion if he were to be seen there on his afternoon off."

"Then we need to find a surprising replacement for you, m'lady. Wouldn't want him to come back to an empty cupboard now, would we?"

"That is a splendid idea, Chief Inspector, but he is without scruples. Anyone posing as me would be in grave danger."

"Don't you worry, I will have men posted all around the basement. We will arrest him as soon as he comes back to get you."

"I wonder…" she said, clasping her hands against her legs. "Since I have established a reputation with Scotland Yard, well…could we possibly come along?"

Two deep lines formed between the chief inspector's raisin brown eyes. "Blood can't speak highly enough of you, and since it is your information that has brought us to this point, I don't see why not—as long as you stay well out of the way."

Dodo jumped up and clapped her hands together. "Thank you, Chief Inspector!"

"I always seem to end up cramped into small, dark quarters with you, m'lady," whispered Lizzie.

"At least there are plenty of policemen around this time." Dodo had underestimated how traumatizing coming back to her prison would be. She was shivering even though Rupert had her firmly clasped to his side.

"True," said Lizzie. "Usually, we are facing a murderer alone."

They were within earshot of the cupboard door but a blanket of policeman was stationed between them and her former place of confinement.

"You do lead an exciting life," murmured Rupert.

"Some would call it that," muttered Lizzie in a salty tone. "I could call it something else."

Dodo wondered how long they would have to wait. Her nerves were half shredded.

The sudden sound of the lift startled her. It was beginning.

She could hear the elevator making its way down to the basement and settle, then the sound of the scissor gate being drawn back. Her heart started thumping.

Quick footsteps cracked along the stone floor and the slim beam of a torch bounced shadows around the walls. She could hear Lizzie's breaths short and fast.

Rupert clutched her hand.

Billy's threatening voice, echoed in the darkness. "Time to go." Reaching for the handle he noticed that the door was open and hurried in. "What the—?"

The bound imposter, a policeman wearing a wig, Dodo's hat and a woman's coat, made muffled sounds of fear through the gag.

"No time for hysterics," shouted Billy as they heard him manhandling the double. "What on earth—?"

A shrill whistle sounded, and all the hidden policemen descended on the closet. Dodo ran forward, an urgent desire to see Billy arrested, overwhelming her fears. A string of expletives flowed from Billy's mouth as he struggled against the arrest. It took several men to confine him.

As he was marched out of the closet, he locked eyes with Dodo.

"You!"

She shuddered and leaned into Rupert.

"You had better watch your back!" he spat out, with the venom of a thousand snakes.

Chapter 23

Dodo was a modern woman who could take care of herself, but the acrimony of Billy's words cut through her like a knife. Perhaps it had been a mistake to insist on being there when he was apprehended. His crazed expression would fill her nightmares for weeks to come.

"She has me to protect her now," yelled Rupert, his voice echoing off the walls and metal machinery.

They watched as the officers dragged away the recalcitrant, cuffed lift attendant.

When he was out of sight, Rupert crushed Dodo to him and kissed her so hard that warmth and fireworks began to push out the fear.

Lizzie covered her eyes again. "Let me know when you're finished," she said, chuckling through her hands.

Just when Dodo thought she could take no more, Rupert pulled away and clamped her in a bear hug, whispering into her hair, "I never want to let you go, my darling."

Several officers had stayed with them in the noisy basement and at length Chief Inspector Morris, having secured the suspect in a prison wagon, came back in search of them.

"Catching the culprit red-handed. Doesn't get any better than that!" His bushy whiskers were moving up and down like a monkey on a hand organ.

"Happy to have helped, Chief Inspector," Dodo said.

"There will be no problem with sending this one away," he continued, sticking his thumbs in his waistcoat and rocking back on his heels.

Though she was happy that Billy had been apprehended, there were still some loose ends. "Will you be trying to find the red-headed man?"

"He is our number one fugitive at this point."

"I'm sorry I don't know his whereabouts," she said. "I don't even know his name."

The smile on the chief inspector's face dwindled. "Lady Dorothea, you have helped us solve two crimes in one fell swoop at considerable danger to yourself: the murder of Miss Stanhope and the drug ring operating out of Livery's. I think that's enough for one day. Let us take care of Ah Lin and the rest."

Haunting jazz was playing on the gramophone, the comforting red, velvet curtains were drawn, a vigorous fire was crackling in the grate and Dodo was wrapped in a soft blanket, laying against Rupert on the sofa while Lizzie toasted muffins in the flames.

They had straggled out of the famous department store just in time to watch the prison wagon haul Billy away.

"To think I nearly went out with a murderer," said Lizzie, her lovely, large eyes reflecting the dancing flames.

"There were two Billys," said Dodo, "the one who invited you out was very pleasant. But I hope there would have been no more dates. I think I will have to do some matchmaking to ensure that we know all about your beaux."

Lizzie shrugged her shoulders. "I don't need a man," she said quietly.

"Watching you with Billy has shown me that you need more experience," said Dodo. "We in the aristocracy are so selfish, we rarely think of the needs of our staff." She reached for Rupert's hand. "It is high time you had your own romance, Lizzie. I shall make it my next case."

All three dissolved into peals of laughter, throwing off the stress of the evening.

"Do you think they will arrest the owner of the opium den?" asked Lizzie.

"I don't know. He didn't murder Stella and opium is not well regulated here…yet. I know they have banned the stuff in America, and it is currently being debated in our own government but as of right now…?" replied Dodo.

"He almost kidnapped Lizzie," Rupert pointed out.

"That's true. You could press charges, Lizzie," said Dodo.

She shook her head vigorously. "I want nothing more to do with that horrid man. Pressing charges will make it linger."

"Well, give it some time."

"The chief inspector is sure that Billy will give up the other people at the store, so depending on their level of involvement, there may be charges," said Rupert.

Lizzie offered him a muffin from the end of her poker. "I still can't get over Billy being a heartless murderer and drug kingpin."

"I know, his friendly act was a great cover," murmured Dodo.

"Do you know why he killed Stella?" asked Lizzie as she impaled another muffin and held it over the fire.

"I asked him," said Dodo in a sleepy voice. "She made the mistake of treating him badly and he came to resent her. From some of the things he said to me, getting rid of inconvenient people was nothing new to him and I imagine he made some pretense of an emergency in the distribution to lure her to Limehouse or something, and confronted her, asking for a bigger slice of the pie. When she refused, he killed her in sight of Ah Lin as a warning."

They sat without talking until the needle on the gramophone began to scratch. Lizzie got up and put another soothing jazz record on.

"By the way, in all the excitement I forgot to mention that my parents called and are staying at an hotel in Surrey to be close to Bea," said Rupert, as he laced his fingers through Dodo's.

"That is wonderful news," cried Dodo. "With support from her family I am sure she can beat this thing."

"They telephoned this afternoon, right before Lizzie, actually."

Dodo sat up to take a bite of the muffin Rupert offered her. "How did they take the news about Beatrice's addiction?"

"They had their suspicions, so it wasn't a complete shock, but they had no idea how bad it was." He bit his cheek. "They still don't know about the shoplifting."

"I don't think they ever need to know, do you?" asked Dodo. "She wasn't responsible, and it is all taken care of."

Rupert wiped a trickle of melted butter from Dodo's chin. "The doctors are hopeful that with the treatment she might be able to go home for Christmas."

"That is wonderful news!" She kicked her legs up under her and rested her head on Rupert's chest. He traced the line of her jaw setting all her nerves dancing.

"Speaking of Christmas," he began sounding less confident. "I was wondering if you would like to spend it with my family in Leicestershire?"

She sat up so that their eyes were aligned. "You want me to meet your family?"

"Would you like to?" His expression held a hint of doubt.

She kissed him lightly, relieved that her ordeal was over, and she was alive to have a future, a future that looked more and more promising.

"I'd like nothing better!"

The End

I hope you enjoyed this cozy mystery, *Murder in Limehouse*, and love Dodo as much as I do.

Interested in a free prequel to this series? Go to https://dl.bookfunnel.com/997vvive24 to download *Mystery at the Derby*.

Book one in the series, *Murder at Farrington Hall* is available on Amazon. https://amzn.to/31WujyS

"Dodo is invited to a weekend party at Farrington Hall. She and her sister are plunged into sleuthing when a murder occurs. Can she solve the crime before Scotland Yard's finest?"

Book two of the series, *Murder is Fashionable* is available on Amazon. https://amzn.to/2HBshwT

"Stylish Dodo Dorchester is a well-known patron of fashion. Hired by the famous Renee Dubois to support her line of French designs, she travels between Paris and London frequently. Arriving for the showing of the Spring 1923 collection, Dodo is thrust into her role as an amateur detective when one of the fashion models is murdered. Working under the radar of the French DCJP Inspector Roget, she follows clues to solve the crime. Will the murderer prove to be the man she has fallen for?"

Book three of the series, *Murder at the Races* is available on Amazon. https://amzn.to/2QIdYKM

"It is royal race day at Ascot, 1923. Lady Dorothea Dorchester, Dodo, has been invited by her childhood friend, Charlie, to an exclusive party in a private box with the added incentive of meeting the King and Queen.
Charlie appears to be interested in something more than friendship when a murder interferes with his plans. The victim is one of the guests from the box and Dodo cannot resist poking around. When Chief Inspector Blood of Scotland Yard is assigned to the case, sparks fly between them again. The chief inspector and Dodo have worked together on a case before and he welcomes her assistance with the prickly upper-class suspects. But where does this leave poor Charlie?

Dodo eagerly works on solving the murder which may have its roots in the distant past. Can she find the killer before they strike again?"

Book four of the series, *Murder on the Moors* is available on Amazon. https://amzn.to/38SDX8d

When you just want to run away and nurse your broken heart but murder comes knocking.

"Lady Dorothea Dorchester, Dodo, flees to her cousins' estate in Dartmoor in search of peace and relaxation after her devastating break-up with Charlie and the awkward attraction to Chief Inspector Blood that caused it.
Horrified to learn that the arch-nemesis from her schooldays, Veronica Shufflebottom, has been invited, Dodo prepares for disappointment. However, all that pales when one of the guests disappears after a ramble on the foggy moors. Presumed dead, Dodo attempts to contact the local police to report the disappearance only to find that someone has tampered with the ancient phone. The infamous moor fog is too thick for safe travel and the guests are therefore stranded.
Can Dodo solve the case without the help of the police before the fog lifts?"

For more information about the series go to my website at www.annsuttonauthor.com and subscribe to my newsletter.

You can also follow me on Facebook at:
https://www.facebook.com/annsuttonauthor

Agatha Christie plunged me into the fabulous world of reading when I was 10. I was never the same. I read every one of her books I could lay my hands on. Mysteries remain my favorite genre to this day - so it was only natural that I would eventually write my own.

Born and raised in England, writing fiction about my homeland keeps me connected.

After finishing my degree in French and Education and raising my family, writing has become a favorite hobby.

I hope that Dame Agatha would enjoy Dodo Dorchester at much as I do.

Acknowledgements

My proof-reader – Tami Stewart

The mother of a large and growing family who reads like the wind with an eagle eye. Thank you for finding little errors that have been missed.

My editor – Jolene Perry of Waypoint Author Academy

Sending my work to editors is the most terrifying part of the process for me but Jolene offers correction and constructive criticism without crushing my fragile ego.

My cheerleader, marketer and IT guy – Todd Matern

A lot of the time during the marketing side of being an author I am running around with my hair on fire. Todd is the yin to my yang. He calms me down and takes over when I am yelling at the computer.

My beta readers – Francesca Matern, Stina Van Cott,

Your reactions to my characters and plot are invaluable.

My critique group – Mary Thomas, Laurie Turner, Lisa McKendrick

For reading my stuff and your helpful suggestions

The Writing Gals and 20Booksto50k for their FB author community and their YouTube tutorials

These sites give so much of their time to teaching their Indie author followers how to succeed in this brave new publishing world. Thank you.

Made in the USA
Las Vegas, NV
22 December 2022